Cries
OF THE
Unknown

Jeannette Amanfo

Copyright © 2023 **JAIM Publishing**

All rights reserved. No part of this publication may be reproduced, distributed, or transmitted in any form or by any means, including photocopying, recording, or other electronic or mechanical methods, without the prior written permission of the publisher, except in the case of brief quotations embodied in critical reviews and certain other noncommercial uses permitted by copyright law. For permission requests, write to the publisher, addressed "Attention: Book Rights and Permission," at the address below.

Published in the United States of America

ISBN 978-1-962569-36-1 (SC)
ISBN 978-1-962569-35-4 (HC)

JAIM Publishing
222 West 6th Street
Suite 400, San Pedro, CA, 90731
www.stellarliterary.com

Ordering Information and Rights Permission:

Quantity sales. Special discounts might be available on quantity purchases by corporations, associations, and others. For details, contact the publisher at the address above.

For Book Rights Adaptation and other Rights Permission. Call us at toll-free 1-888-945-8513 or send us an email at admin@stellarliterary.com.

Contents

1 1
2 14
3 21
4 31
5 39
6 47
7 56
8 64
9 72
10 82
11 89
12 101
13 109
14 118
15 125
16 133
17 142
18 149
19 157

1

TRAFFICKING

This is a story about April who is called Cookie by her kidnappers, who was kidnapped at seven years old and forced into a life of Sex trafficking.

We will start by telling the story of Cookie, a young lady that is now nine years old, when she was the young age of seven years old, she was kidnapped by a terrible wicked man who goes by the name of Dominic Hernandez. Dominic picked her up as she was walking home from school the year of 2021.

She never knew what life was going to be for her from that day forward. She had plans to go home to her mother and little brother and make some cookies together. She thought how ironic it was that her kidnapper happened to start calling her the name Cookie, from the very beginning, instead of by her given name her mother and father had gave to her at the time of birth, April Davis. She sat in the back seat with her hands tied together and her mouth taped shut. Tears of fear fell down her little face as she was thinking what she was going through was just a terrible dream. She closed her eyes, tightly, in hopes of when they opened it would be where she was safe and at her home.

It seemed like they drove for many hours. She had fallen to sleep at one point and woke up with it being dark outside, and still the evil man was driving.

At one point she felt like she would pee her pants, not being able to use a bathroom anywhere. She felt so hungry, knowing that she was in the man's car for several hours, and no food or water was offered to her.

"Now Cookie, you come with me, I will be dropping you off here, this will be your new home from here on out." He pulled her by the rope that had her hands tied.

As she followed him by the rope that she was tied too, she looked around her, to see if she might have known the place from somewhere she might have been to at one point. She could see an old building that looked dark and so scary for her. A place she had never seen before now. It was dark out and she could barely make it out what it looked like. As she was forced into the building, it carried a strong smell, one of which she hated right away. *"What is this place?"* she asked herself seeing several men looking her direction. Then she heard them speak a language she didn't know. They all seemed to be darker than she was, and she never knew any of them. She stood there still tied, and her mouth covered so she couldn't let out screams in hopes that someone would hear her and come to her rescue. She watched as a big man, approached her and looked down at her. He looked so big to her standing in front of her, fear shook her to the very core of her beings.

He ripped the tape off of her mouth, it hurt her so bad, that fear alone caused her to pee her pants. She stood there feeling so frightened, that her little framed body began to shake and quiver.

"She just pissed her pants." He spoke looking at the man that brought her in the place.

The wicked man that kidnapped her slapped her across her little face. "What do you think that you're doing, you stand here and pee just like that."

Cookie was crying so hard she could hardly breathe, she just wanted to go home, and see her mom. One of the men grabbed ahold of her by the rope, and started to walk her in a dark hallway.

"I'll show you to your room."

As she was passing the other rooms, that were closed with curtains hanging, she could hear the cries of others coming from behind them. She was scared for herself and for the cries of the unknown.

"Now I want you to change out of them clothes, and if you want something to eat, then you better do what you are told, or you will go hungry." The man told her. He untied her hands and threw some clothes at her. He was ready to walk out, then looked back at her. "In case you're thinking about trying to escape us here, you better think again. You belong to me now, I just paid good money for you." He turned and walked out the curtain.

Cookie stood there scared to death of what next was going to happen to her. Who were these mean men that are forcing her to stay in the dirty place, against her will. She picked up a dress that the man threw at her, she looked around her surrounding to see what was in the room where they brought her. She seen a bed, all messed up, nothing clean and tidy like at her home. There were no windows to look outside, it was stinky and a dirty place. She put on the dress that looked like it belonged to someone several years older than herself. She sat down on the bed, which was very uncomfortable to her. Everything she seen was uncomfortable, nothing was like she was used too. She laid down in a fetal position. She tried not to cry, she didn't want anyone coming back in and hurt her, or make her cry all the more.

She felt so tried, but was afraid to sleep, afraid of what might happen to her if she was to sleep. She laid there with her eyes wide open, thinking about her mom and dad, and little brother. Would she ever see them again, would life ever make sense again. Were these men planning on killing her, or what was their plan.

Cookie fell to sleep while fighting it. She was woken up when a lady came in the room. "Cookie," the women spoke. "My name is Tina, I will be the one to come in and make sure that you get your food and water, and also, if you are good, and do what your told, then you will get to bathe, a couple times a week."

She listened to the women talk, wondering if she would help her get home, all she wanted was her mom.

"Cookie, are you listening to me?" the lady took a hold of her face and gave it a light squeeze.

She shook her head yes.

"Okay, I am going to ask you a couple of questions now, so I need you to answer me, okay?"

Cookie was so scared; she shook her head yes again.

"Cookie, I don't want you shaking your head yes or no, I want you to answer me yes or no. Do I make myself clear."

"Yes."

"My first question to you, have you ever been with a man before?"

She wondered why the lady was asking her that kind of a question. "No." she was so scared with just hearing a question like that.

Being so young, she didn't understand the meaning. She knew that she has been with her dad and uncles before.

"Okay, this place is a place where you will meet many men, they will come in here, and they will want to be with you.

Now, I want you to just allow them to have their way with you, I will be expecting you to behave yourself like a young lady, so there will be no crying, no wanting to go home. This is your home now, and this is your new life."

Cookie started to cry, at the thoughts of someone coming in to see her that she didn't know, and her mother not being there to protect her was so scary.

"You must stop crying; I told you that if you don't listen you will not get anything to eat. So, I am going to be sending in the first man to see you, and I want you to behave yourself."

She stood up to walk out of the room.

Cookie sat on the bed crying and scared, all she wanted was to go home. She wondered what her mom and dad were doing now, that she was no longer home with them. Had they called the police up, have they told family members that she was missing? She heard someone coming down the hallway, she sat up straight, and looked towards the curtain. Her heart began to race so fast, she felt like it was going to leave her whole body.

A man opened the curtain and looked at her sitting in the bed crying. "Hello Cookie, my name is Azra, how are you doing tonight?" he sat next to her. "I here that you are a new girl here brought in just today, well I guess you were told, what your job is to be doing for us, am I right?"

Cookie wasn't sure how to answer that question, she never knew it was called a job, so she never answered the man.

"Okay, well I will be the first man that you will be with, so I need you to take off your dress."

When she heard what he wanted from her, she grabbed ahold of her arms and held herself tight. She didn't want to remove her clothes, she was always taught at home, never to allow anyone but your husband to see you naked.

The man took a hold of her hands, and pulled them loose from holding so tight on her arms. "It's okay, come on let's get it off of you, then I want you to just lay down and relax." He stood her up in front of him, as he sat down on the bed, he slowly removed them from her, all the while she was crying and wondered what he was going to do to her.

After her clothes were removed, he laid her back on the bed, and he removed his clothes.

Cookie could not believe what was happening to her, her whole life is making no sense to her. One minute she had a wonderful family, one that took good care of her, they loved her and taught her to love others. But now she had a big older man around the age of forty years old, raping her. This man was hurting her so bad; he must be someone's dad, but why would he abuse a young girl. Inside of her, she began to scream, she felt like she was about to lose her mind, and never get it back. She felt like she was being torn apart, he was hurting her worse than she had even been hurt.

After the man was done, he got up and put his clothes back on. He walked out without saying a word to her. She asked herself, "why he never said that he was sorry, did he have no remorse for what he did?" She laid there, weeping, and she felt so dirty for what happened to her. Her bottom hurt so badly, she didn't know if she would ever feel good again. She wondered why the man grabbed her when she was walking home from school, when there were so many other girls that were walking home, but the bad man grabbed her. "Was he mad at someone in her family? Did he and her dad get mad at each other?" Question after question flooded her mind, she wanted to know what she did wrong.

She had blood all over on her bed, and she was too sick to get up out of the blood. She couldn't understand why this sort of thing was happening to her and the others she heard crying.

"Cookie." Tina walked back into the room, seeing that blood was all over on the bed.

Cookie looked at her while still laying down, she hoped that after seeing what happened to her, that Tina would help her go back home to her family.

"Cookie, I need you to get up, I need to get your bed cleaned up. I want you to go into the bathroom down the hallway, and clean yourself up."

She pulled her by the arm, and forced her to get up. "I want you to follow me, there is a bathtub, you will need to get in there and wash this blood off from you. Wash your hair too, I can see some blood is in there too. After your bath, I will bring you in something to eat." She took her by the hand and stood her up. "Follow me."

Cookie hurt to walk, and she never bothered to say anything to Tina. But she had thoughts going through her head that was not so nice about the woman.

"Here is a clean towel and wash cloth. Here is some shampoo, and soap. Make sure to wash all of you, because after you eat, we have a job for you to do." She walked out of the bathroom leaving Cookie to take her bath.

Cookie started to run some bath water, all the while she cried from the pain she felt. She climbed in the tub, and sat down in the warm water. It stung her to even sit, but she knew she needed to wash off the blood, and also wash it out of her hair.

She sat in the tub crying for her mother. She wondered if the police were out looking for her. She sat in the tub daydreaming about her family, when she heard a loud knock on the door.

"Come on out of there now." A man's voice yelled.

After she was all washed up, she got out and dressed in the clothes that Tina gave to her to put on. She opened the door slowly to the bathroom, not knowing who was on the outside of it waiting for her.

"Cookie, go to your room, I will bring you in some food." Tina spoke.

She walked down the hallway to her room, she sat down on the bed, anticipating what she was going to eat and hopefully drink. She hadn't eaten anything since when she was last at school. She was very hungry and thirsty. She remembered what she was told, if she would do as she was told, then she could eat.

It wasn't long before Tina brought her back a plate of food. She handed it to Cookie. "Now you can have more just like this if you will continue to listen to what we say. Do I make myself clear?"

Just hearing her voice ran shivers down her spine. "Yes." She said as she looked what she had on her plate. Tina walked out of the room, leaving Cookie to eat her food. She picked up a sandwich that was there, and took a big bite. Pulling it away from her and looking at what kind it was. She didn't even know, but took another bite, because she was so hungry, it didn't matter what kind it was, as long as it was food, she was eating it. She could see that there was also rice and beans on her plate. She hurried and ate that up as well. After eating her food, she felt a little sick to her stomach. Laying down on her bed, she laid with her knees brought up close to her belly, in hopes that what she felt would go away.

Tina came back to gather the plate from her, when she noticed that Cookie was feeling unwell. "What's wrong with you?" she asked staring down at the child.

"I don't feel good, my stomach hurts."

"Why would it hurt, I just went out of my way to make sure that you were given good food."

Cookie didn't know what to say about that. She just laid there holding her stomach.

"Cookie, if you don't stop this right now, then Kevin will be very angry with you. You have a job to do, and if it doesn't get done, Kevin will have my hide."

Cookie tried sitting up, she didn't want him to come back and hurt her, although she felt sick, she sat up.

"That's my girl. Now you just do your job, and I will make sure that you get food."

She thought that it was the food that made her sick, it's not something that she wanted to eat anymore. Maybe she got sick, because she ate it so fast, maybe because it was the first time eating in a day. She sat on the edge of her bed, when she noticed the curtain open up. Seeing a tall dark man walk in and look down at her.

"You're just a little thing they have here. Well, lets get on with it then."

She wasn't sure what he was asking from her, saying let's get on with it. She sat there hoping for her stomach ache to go away.

"Come child, take my clothes off of me." He demanded.

The thoughts that a grown man wanted her to remove his clothes was enough to make her sick, on top of how she was already feeling. She looked up at him, with questioning eyes.

"Come on, I want you to remove my clothes for me."

She stood up like she was asked. Standing in front of him, her size was so small compared to his size. How would she get this big mans clothes off of him, was beyond her. She looked up at him, not sure what she was supposed to do.

"Undo my pants for me." He told her.

She hated the feeling that she was getting, fear hit her all through her little body. She felt like she would throw-up. She tried to undo his button on his pants. But it was too hard, she looked up at him, with tears coming down her cheeks. She was afraid of what he was going to do to her, if she couldn't remove his clothes for him.

He could tell that she was not strong enough to remove them, he had a belly that hung over top of his pants, and he was expecting a small child to take them off of him. He sat her down, and he removed them himself, then he sat down on the bed. "Stand up child."

She stood up, not wanting to look at the naked man.

He pulled her in front of him. "Remove your clothes."

She started to shed more tears, she hated what was happening to her, she wanted her mother.

"I asked that you remove them right now."

Cookie started to take off her clothes, and let them fall to the floor. She tried covering herself up the best that she could.

He removed both of her hands, and placed them down next to her side.

She stood there feeling so ashamed that a man was now staring at her little naked body. Something her mother told her that only a husband was to see.

The man pulled her in close to him, forcing her to sit on his lap. Cookie began to scream in pain that she was feeling, until she seen no more.

She woke up sometime later, unaware of what happened to her. She was in her bed, with the covers pulled over her body. She remembered the man that came in to see her, she didn't know if it was him that covered her or someone else.

Tina came in to check on her. "Cookie, are you awake now?" she asked knowing that the room was very dark at the time.

Cookie tried to pretend that she was still sleeping, she thought that maybe Tina wanted to bring another man in to see her, and he too would hurt her beyond anything imaginable.

Tine walked over to her. "Cookie" she snapped.

She opened her eyes, and looked up at Tina, now she was able to see that Tina turned a light on, and could see her. "Yes." She spoke in a weak weary voice.

"I have someone that wants to come in and see you. I need you to sit up, you must behave yourself if you're going to want to eat."

Cookie wanted to die, she hated these men coming in and hurting her. She knew what they were doing to her and all the other children there, it was evil in every way.

"Come on, I allowed you to sleep for a while to gather yourself. Now its time that you earn us some money. Kevin paid a lot of money for you; he wants his money's worth. Sit up." She demanded.

Cookie could hear the wickedness in Tina's voice, she knew that she was just as bad as all the men that came in to hurt her. She sat up, feeling like she wanted to just die, so she never had to feel pain like that again.

Another man came in to see her, then another. She didn't know when all of this evil would ever come to an end. After several hours had gone by, she was not sure of the time, but she knew it was late. A day had gone by, and another day began.

Night time came, and she was very hungry, she could hear the screams of others coming from behind the walls and curtains. "What is happening to them? Are they being raped and abused too? Was it the same man that did that to her?"

Tina came in to talk with her. "Cookie, okay you fulfilled your first tasks for the day, we are on the second day now, I will bring you in something to eat. Would you like that?" she could tell that Cookie was frightened about another man coming in to see her.

"The last stuff you brought me, made me feel sick." She spoke afraid of getting the same thing.

"Okay, I will bring you another plate of food."She stood up and ready to walked out. "It will be different then the first one.

Cookie felt so alone, so afraid. "Why would anyone do this sort of thing to another person, especially a child." She wondered. She felt so hungry, the last time she ate anything is when she got sick.

Tina brought her in some food in a bowl. Cookie wondered why she told her that she was going to get a plate of food, but it was only a bowl of something that looked like slop. She was so hungry, she took the bowl. She knew not to question her what it was, or where the plate of food was. She started to eat the food, she didn't get much, nothing like when she was home by any means. After eating most of what she was given, she began to feel drowsy. She didn't know what was going on with her, and Tina sat there staring at her as she began to close her eyes.

She didn't know how long she was sleeping, but she woke up, alone and afraid. She knew that she was having a terrible night-mare, one of which all she wanted was to wake up from it.

Everything was quiet at the moment, she wanted to look on the outside of the curtain, but she was too afraid. She laid there, staring at the curtain, to see if it was going to move again, or maybe open up to another man walking in and hurting her again.

After laying there in one spot without moving an inch, she peeled herself off the bed, and tip-toed to the curtain. Standing there before attempting to open it up, she listened to hear if anyone might have been out there.

Sneaking a little peek, she looked where only one eye could see outside of her three walls. She couldn't see anything, or hear anything. Then she noticed another young girl walking back into room. *"Who is that?"* she wondered. Watching to see if she could see the other girl again, or anyone coming down the hallway. She stood very still, afraid to move, that it might make a noise.

She stared at the curtain that the other girl was held behind. Finally, after her not seeing anyone come for quite a while, she tip-toed across the narrow hallway, and peeked through the girl's curtain. Seeing her lying in bed, she noticed the girl look at her. At first, she jumped back, but then she could see the girl was sobbing quietly. Cookie looked down the hallway again hoping not to be seen. She walked in the room, "are you okay?"

"I want my mom." She sobbed.

"I want mine too. How long have you been here?" Cookie asked.

"I don't know, but I hate these people, they are mean and hurt me every day."

Cookie hated to hear where they hurt her every day, that meant that they were going to do the same to her too. "I just got here yesterday, and I want to go home." She heard a noise, she hurried and rushed back to her room, before she was caught. Crawling into her bed, she closed her eyes, acting like she was asleep.

She stayed in bed, falling to sleep thinking about what the girl across the hallway said about being abused every day. Cookie hurt all over, she felt like a Mack truck had run her over she didn't feel very good. When she woke up in the morning, who could she tell that she was unwell. Who would care that she was sick? Would they help her or care to get her feeling better? She knew that she needed to get cleaned up, but how, she didn't know how to get to the bathroom on her own. As it was, she used a corner in her room to go to the toilet. No one came in to show her how to get to the bathroom when she needed too. Now her room had a worse smell in there then it had when she came in the day before.

She sat on the edge of her bed, afraid for what was coming her way again today. She had only eaten twice, since she came there, and she didn't even know what it was they gave to her.

Her belly was hungry, she missed her family, her home, and her bed. She even missed the dog they had, when she never cared for him when she was at home. But seeing little buddy now would be a breath of fresh air compared to what is going on in her life now.

"Am I ever going to see my family again, is this all my life will be like forever until I die?" her thoughts began to flood on all the what if's.

It seemed like she sat there half the day before someone came in the room to say something to her. She seen the curtain open up, it was the man that brought her to the room, Kevin the one that said he paid a lot of money for her, the one that said she better not try and run away. Fear struck her deep inside of her.

"Are you hungry?" the man asked her.

She shook her head yes, instead of saying yes.

"We don't hear head shaking, we hear words spoken. Are you hungry?" he asked the second time, looking at her like he was the devil.

She was so afraid of the man, she shook her head, while saying "yes."

"Okay, I have someone here to see you for a while, if you will perform your duties, then afterwards, you will be able to eat. Do I make myself clear?"

She hated the thoughts of another nasty stinking man come in her room and hurt her again. "Why?" she spoke.

"You want to eat, don't you?" he looked at her angry.

"Yes."

"Around here, in order to eat, you work for what you are going to eat."

She sat there not saying another word, her heart felt like it was just going to die, instead of beating like it had been for the last seven years it would suddenly stop. She was too afraid to speak, what monster was going to come into her smelly nasty dark room, and abuse her next?

She watched him give her the final warning about behaving herself and doing her job well, then he walked out of the room. She waited for the next man to enter the room, if only she could disappear before he came in. If only he would save her and take her home to her parents, instead of harming her like the other ones did. All the wishful thinking was just what it was, wishful thinking, she watched as a man came in her room, he was not as old as the first few were, but it was still another abuser. He had no interest in helping her get free from the house of horror and pain. He was one of the evil people that come to tear a child up with his vicious attacks against their little bodies.

She could not fight him off if she tried, but the whole time in her mind, she was crying and screaming please someone save me, get me out of here.

2

Cookie, was taken away from everyone she loved, now more than two weeks ago, her life that she has become to know now, was pure hell. She had been beaten by the men that would rape her, she was left without eating for up to two days at a time. Her life was nothing but pure evil being done to her.

She was told that if she did not perform to the man's needs, then she would face great punishment, and she had.

She was learning to do what was expected of her, trying to do it the way she was told. She knew that soon she would be turning eight years old, and she would not be at home to celebrate it with family.

The little girl that she spoke to that one night, she remembered seeing her one last time, when two men were carrying out her body. She didn't know if she was beaten to death, or starved to death. All she knew is that she seen her limp body being taken out by two mean men, and she never seen her again, or heard her cries.

Cookie was beginning to feel so much turmoil inside of her that she began to cut herself with a fork, when food was brought into her. She wanted to die, she didn't have the will to fight or live anymore. The thoughts of all these evil men coming in and laying down on her small little body, sickened her.

Each day that went by, she wanted to end her pain, she just wanted to leave her body, and disappear. Fearing that she would never see her family or friends again, fearing that this was all that life was for her now, she decided that she was going to take her own life.

After another man came into her, she was able to eat something. She had a tight grip on the fork, and began to cut at her wrist, she wanted to end her pain, stop the abuse from continuing. She kept cutting, and seeing the blood start to flow out of her wrist. She started to feel light headed, she woke up sometime later, in her room, with her wrist all bandaged up.

"What do you think that you were doing?" Snapped Tina when she came in her room before, telling her what her job would be if she wanted to eat.

She didn't know what to say to the woman, she was afraid of being beat again, if she said the wrong thing.

"I think that you need to say something to me, or else I will have to get one of the men to come in here and punish you."

She tried to think of what she could say, but didn't know how to spit it out. Tears began to drip down her cheeks. "I want to go home." Is all that came out.

The lady had no compassion on her at all, she squeezed her arm tightly. "This is your home; you need to get it out of your head that there is another place for you. It was your parents that told us to take you, they didn't want you anymore." She let go of her arm. "Do I make myself clear?"

Cookie knew that this woman had no good in her, she didn't care to help her at all. She was in to making her do the unthinkable acts with men of all ages. Small, fat, skinny, tall. Black, white, Mexican, it didn't matter to them, they all came to see and abuse cookie.

One day she overheard talk between the man that bought her, and a lawyer, when she was let out of her room, to go to the bathroom to clean up. She stood with her ear up by the door, to hear what was being said.

"She's in the bathroom now, just give it a few minutes and I will have her back in her room."

She knew that they must have been referring to her. She was the one in the bathroom. She had never known lawyers to do this kind of thing, why would he be coming in to see me. *"Did these evil people get me a lawyer, and why would they do that, when they are the ones that have hurt me?"* she began to question if someone had a good heart and had a lawyer come out to help her get back home.

She heard a knock on the bathroom door. "Hurry up in there."

She jumped, at the knock, and then opened the door. She seen the mean man that paid money for her, standing there waiting. He grabbed ahold of her roughly. "Get to your room, you have a visitor."

She felt her heart skip a beat, *"A visitor, it has to be the lawyer, he's come to help me to be able to go home."* She felt so excited, she hurried down the hallway, excited that something good was finally coming for her.

She sat on her bed, waiting to see the lawyer, she was trying to think what kind of questions that he would ask her, what would she say to him, to get him to take her home. She never believed a word the lady told her when she said that her parents never wanted her and wanted them to take her and bring her here.

She watched as the man walked in and looked at her for a minute before speaking to her. He seen a small child, one that looked broken and empty, one that longed to get free of the hell that she was going through. He smiled at her, giving her a small sign of hope.

She gave him a weak smile back. "Did you come here to take me home?" she asked hoping that was the case.

He looked at her and gave her a grin, but the grin was not one that she was expecting to get from him, it was an evil grin, one that said she was mistaking badly. Fear gripped her very soul, she knew that he was not her to help her at all, she knew that he was there to hurt her just like all the others did.

"No, I'm not taking you home today, but maybe another day I will be able to take you." He sat next to her on the bed. I think it's time that we get down to business, I have places to go, so I guess you know the routine, I take it you been here for a while now."

She had tears form in her eyes; fear gripped her once again. Would the pain ever leave and never come back? She sat there not budging, nor removing her clothes from him, or her. She knew that some of the men that came to see her, like it when she would undress them as well as herself.

After he seen that she was not going to do what she was supposed to do, he removed his clothes, and then hers. She tried to block out everything that she was going through, she hated what evil was taking place.

After he was done, he dressed and looked at her. "I'll see about getting you out of here so you can go home."

She had a small hope build up on the inside of her over the course of several days, after he left. Each time someone came in to see her, she was hoping it would be that lawyer with the news he was taking her out of there and taking her back to her parents.

She wondered how her family was doing? Did they still think about her, are they putting up signs all over looking for her. She has not seen the outside of the place since she was brought there. How she longed to see the trees and the shy, to look at the grass, and run through it again like she used to at her home. There were times that she could no longer see the faces of her family when she tried too. But then other times, she could barely make them out. She was losing hope of ever seeing them again, and wondered if they knew what she had been doing, would they even want her back.

She did what she was told, and each time she went to the bathroom, she could see herself in the mirror, and she noticed that she was thin and didn't look healthy. She knew the only way she would eat, is if she never put up a fuss about having men come in to see her, and she have sex with them anyway they wanted it.

One day, the man that bought her, came in and told her that he wanted her to talk with another girl that was just brought in that day. He said that she was a nine-year-old girl, and it was her job to coach her into doing all the things that she had been doing since she arrived there. Cookie never wanted to do anything like that at all, she knew the pain and evil that was being done to her every day, often times fifty-sixty times a day.

She hated the thoughts of these men bringing little girls into the place just to be hurt and abused by men.

"Cookie, I will be taking you to her room, there you will talk with her about her job, do I make myself clear?"

She looked at him, wanting to say no, but she knew if she didn't do what she was told, then she would have hell to pay for being disobedient. "Okay" she finally got to come out of her mouth.

"Okay, follow me."

She stood up, reluctantly following him. She hated the thoughts of telling the girl to sleep with men and that everything was going to be okay. She knew that it was not okay, she knew the terrible things that they would do to her, and not give her food if she refused to do what she was told. She knew the mind abuse, was terrible, she knew the slaps and bruising's were terrible. What could she say to soften it for the girl. She hated what these men were doing to her and others.

"Now you tell her what her job is, and I don't want any foolishness from either of you." She watched as Kevin walked out of the closed curtain. Cookie looked at the little girl, smaller than she was when she came in a few weeks ago. She could see the look of fear in her eyes when she looked at her, her heart sunk in the bottom of her chest. She knew what she was ordered to do, but how can she do that, how does she tell her what her life was just about to become.She walked over to her, and sat down on the bed. First thing she did was hug the girl. "What's your name?"

"Toni." She spoke in a weak voice.

"My name is April, but they call me Cookie. I hate this place, and I want to go home. I'm sure you want to go home too."

She shook her head yes.

"I have to tell you some things, they are making me tell you. I don't want to tell you anything, I want you and me to be able to go home. But if I don't tell you, they will beat me very bad."

Toni looked at her. "They beat you?"

"Yes, I've been very badly beaten a few times, I've went without any food for a couple of days. If you don't do what they tell you to do, they will starve you, and beat you."

"What are we supposed to do?" she asked scared to even ask.

"They bring men in to see us." She could tell that Toni did not understand what that even meant.

"Why?"

"They hurt us very bad, they sleep with us. Do you know what rape means?" she asked her because she didn't even know if she understood the meaning.

"It's where someone forces you to do something in bed that you don't want to do."

"Yes, that's what they do to us here." Cookie noticed someone standing on the outside of the curtain. She knew that she needed to fill in more detail to Toni. "Toni, if you want to eat, and not die of hunger, you need to let these men have sex with you."

"No, I don't want that, my mom will be mad at me if I let anyone touch me."

Cookie wanted to cry for her, she knew that she just was not seeing the bigger picture. She didn't know what else to say to her, she did what she was told to do, she told her what they would want from her in order to eat. "I'm so sorry they caught you, I've been here for weeks now, I'm not even sure how long, but I want to go home, I hate this place." After she said that, Kevin came in and sent her back to her room.

After walking out of Toni's room, Cookie broke down crying. She hurt deep inside; beyond anything she could have even imagined. Sitting on her bed, and bringing her knees up to her face, she fell into them weeping loudly, and uncontrollably.

Kevin heard her crying, and got very upset with her. He expected more from her, he knew that she knew the rules by now, and he expected her to do everything that she was commanded to do. "You really disappoint me." he yelled at her.

Cookie, looked up at him, not knowing what was going to come next. "I gave you one little simple assignment to do, and you could not fulfill what you were told."

She was deeply afraid at this ugly beast of a man. "I told her, if she wanted to eat, she would have to sleep with men. I told her that she will be beaten if she didn't listen to you. I did what you told me to do." She stuttered.

"I never told you to tell her how much you hated this place, and how you want to go home. This is your home." He yelled. "I told you before, I own you, you will never see your family again, this here is your life now. If I ever hear you tell another that you hate this place, and you want to go home, I will cut you up into little pieces, and scatter your body parts all over the place."

She could see in his eyes, there was nothing but pure evil. She was more afraid of him, than she ever has been before.

He walked over to her and grabbed her by the neck, he began to squeeze it tightly, to where she thought that she was going to die. She tried fighting him, she grabbed ahold of his hands as they were wrapped around her neck. Until she seen no more, darkness came in. She woke up some time later, remembering what happened to her. She remembered the feeling just before she passed out, thinking this was all over for her, she was going to die, and would never see her family again.

She laid in bed, not knowing how long she had been knocked out. Sitting up in bed, she felt like her breath was bring taken from her.

It wasn't long for her to be sitting there when she heard the loudest scream coming from Toni's room. She just knew that it was coming from her room without seeing it for herself. Cookie covered her ears, just to hear the torment coming from her room, she knew what was happening to her. She hated these people; she hated the evil that they were doing to the girls. She cried for her, she cried for all the others that she could hear their pain, when it was their first time being raped. She knew the first time being with a man, was always the worse.

All she wanted was to go home, and see every child there to be able to go home. There would be many men coming and going raping her, some wanted more than just sex, they wanted oral sex from her. She wanted death for these evil men, how can they do what they do.

3

Cookie had been there for about a year now, she was unsure just how long, she even was unsure of her age now.

As time went on, she seen many children being brought in from these evil men and even some women. She witnessed the killing of some of the children that tried to fight off their predators.

She witnessed where one little girl was punched to death, beaten by the hands of her owner. The child fought all the way, until her little body went limp, and never moved again. Two men picked her up, and carried her body out. She never knew where they took the bodies of the ones that had died. All she knew is if she wanted to live to see her family again, she needed to do what she was told. She tried to keep the memories of her family alive in her, although they seemed to grow faint.

There were times that two men came in to see her at once, those were times she wished death would come to her. She would rather die, then go through the torture of having these nasty men repeatedly raping her. It was like she was just a no body, a big nothing, no good to anyone.

Fuzzy, a little girl across the hallway came into Cookies room during the night while others were sleeping. She asked Cookie if there was anyway, they could escape while people were sleeping. Cookie knew they could not escape; the doors were all chained and bolted.

"Cookie, please let's go tonight." She begged.

"Shhh, we cannot go, they are all bolted with chains on the doors. They only have keys to unlock them." She didn't want anyone to hear them talking. "Travis is a very mean man, and I'd hate for him to catch you in my room. He might hurt the both of us, now please go back to your room, very quietly."

She watched as Fuzzy walked out of her room tip toeing. She hurt for her, she often could hear her crying, and there was nothing that she could do to save her or even help her. She wished there was a way to escape, she would take everyone that had been kidnapped with her.

Morning came all too soon, there were the days that all she wanted was to sleep and never wake up again, unless it was in her parent's home.

When men weren't coming in and out throughout the day, she would lay in bed and imagine returning home to her family. No matter how much the bad people told her that her family hated her and wanted her gone, she refused to believe them.

One day she walked out of her room, to go use the bathroom, when she seen there were three little boys with ropes around their wrist, they were made to follow Travis down the hallway. She never knew there were boys there until that time. She wondered what were they planning on doing with little boys. She knew that a man will be with a girl, but were there going to be ladies come in to see the boys, she wondered.

Cookie's life was mixed up and confused. She hated her life, and everyone in the place except the children.

It was a few days after the boys arrived that they brought one of the little boys out of his room to go and get cleaned up in the bathroom. Cookie knew as soon as she seen him, that he had been severely abused, he was bleeding from his butt. She started to cry, his eyes were black and blue, they looked all sunk in, he looked like at any time he would fall over dead. Something became enraged on the inside of her, she stood in the hallway, and started to scream as loud as she could, the screams continued going until Kevin came running down the hallway after her. It felt like she just lost her mind, she couldn't hold herself back from exploding any longer. Kevin grabbed ahold of her arm, and drug her back to her room. All the while he was dragging her, she kept screaming.

Later that evening, Travis, Kevin's second-hand man in charge, came in and beat her almost with an inch of her life. Cookie was beaten badly, to where they didn't know if she was going live or die. Kevin was angry with Travis for coming so close to killing her. Cookie was the number one girl that the men liked to see, she made them the most money.

It was nearly three weeks before she was well enough for anyone to come and see her. She needed to have much healing before she could be touched, after Travis broke some of her ribs.

Once she was healed, she was wishing that Travis would have just killed her. She knew that she would be beaten again and again if she didn't listen to orders. If she refused to give many men what they wanted, she would be forced violently, and have to go days without food, and at times no water to drink. She would cry out to die, how she wanted death, over the life that she was forced into.

Time kept going no matter how she wanted it to end. Her whole life has become no good. When she was home, she remembered how her family all loved each other. She remembered the day when her mother was going to be having her younger brother, how she couldn't wait to be a big sister. She knew that she would love him and protect him, keep him safe from getting hurt. She laid in bed, remembering the smell of her home, it was a sweet smell, her mother always had good smells coming from having plug ins in the electricalsockets. But now all she smelled was like the smell of death, it stunk, she hated to have to smell it every day. She wanted to see her family again, before they kill her, every day she could feel they were getting that much closer to killing her.

Kevin came back in the room to talk with her. "Cookie, how are you feeling today?"

She had never had him ask her how she was doing before, this was all new for her. She wasn't sure how to even answer him, after never hearing that from him before. So, she didn't answer him, she just looked at him.

"Travis was out on line when he did what he did to you. I have had a stern talk with him."

She listened to him talk, all the while she was thinking, a stern talk, what does that even mean, you all are wicked to all of us here. She had been there for more then two years now, and Kevin had never spoken nice to her before.

"Cookie, I am going to start letting you do other things, it will get you out of here for a while every day."

When she heard get her out, her eyes opened wide. "What do you mean?" anything would be better than staying in a dark place every day all day. It's been a long time since she had seen the outside, she wanted to see it so badly, and breathe in fresh air.

"You will be able to go outside once a day for a little while.

You are looking sickly, and Tina said its because you never see the outside anymore. She feels this will help you start feeling better.

Cookie was thinking getting to go home would make her feel better, but she kept her thoughts to herself.

"I'm going to send you out with some of the other girls. They will keep an eye on you while your outside.

Cookie knew that the whole time she had been there, she had only spoken with two of the girls. Both of them cried all the times, one of them lost her life.

These girls will watch over you, until someone comes and picks you up."

She didn't know what he meant by someone picking her up.

"Who is going to pick me up?" she asked not understanding. She just thought that he said he was going to let her go outside to be able to get fresh air, now he is saying someone will pick her up.

"The girls that I allow to go outside, are also the ones that have men that want to take you out and show you a good time. After they have completed their time with you, they will bring you back here."

Cookie didn't know if that was a good thing or not, she didn't know what he meant by taking them out and showing them a good time. She had many thoughts going through her head, but she also kept them to herself.

"I want you to go into the bathroom, get yourself cleaned up, you will be going outside soon."

She listened to him and decided not to ask to many questions. She wanted to get to the outside of these dark walls so bad, that she was willing to do anything to get outside and hope for the best.

After reaching the bathroom, Tina was waiting for her. "Cookie, now tonight is a very import time for you. I have some nice clothes for you to put on, and also, I will be putting some makeup on you after you get the clothes on you."

She listened to what Tina was saying, but she had never worn any makeup before. Why would she need to wear makeup, only ladies did that or the older girls. But she was not about to start asking any questions. "Okay." She spoke.

She went into the bathroom, anticipating going outside, although she knew there would not be daylight for much longer. But to be able to smell the air once again, made her feel happy inside. She opened the door after her clothes were put on. "I'm done." She spoke looking at Tina talking with a man across the hallway.

This man was a good looking young black man. What was he doing here? He didn't look like the others that came in here to rape the boys and girls. He had a kind face, but what would he be doing in such a terrible place?

Tina walked back over to her, "okay go back into the bathroom, I will put some makeup on you now."

Cookie listened; she went back in after she noticed that nice looking young man was staring at her.

"Cookie, did you see that man standing out there that I was talking with?"

"Yes." She spoke as Tina was putting eyeshadow on her.

"That is the man that wants to take you out tonight. He wants to be able to spend some time with you alone, out of this place." She looked at Cookie to see what she might think. "Maybe he will take you to get some good food to eat, and then maybe a hotel somewhere."

When she heard take her to a hotel, she already hated the man. He didn't look like he was one of the others, but now she knew he was just the same as they were. She knew the fear she was having about the man was not going to do her any good. She had no control of what happened to her. She was not the boss of her own life or body.

"Okay, we don't want to keep him waiting longer than he has too. Let's get out there, and I want you to put a big smile on your face."

"A smile, I hate to smile at these wicked men, I hate them so much." She thought to herself, but she knew that she better do what she was told to

do. She didn't understand why a man came inside to pick her up, when she was told that she would go outside with some of the other girls. She walked outside of the bathroom, facing the man that stood there waiting for her. She managed to put a slight smile on her face, but behind the smile were tears of pain. She just knew what was coming to her, all she could do was look forward to going outside, and smelling the fresh air. She stood before him; hello my name is Cookie." Tina told her that was a must for her to do.

"How about you and I taking a drive?"

"Okay."

"Okay, lets go." He took her by the arm and led her out of the place.

Cookie's heart raced so fast not knowing what was expected of her. When first stepping outside, she could see the beautiful sky, something she had not seen since she was brought to this terrible place. She took a deep breath in, it felt so good to be able to breathe like that again.

"Are you okay?" the man asked seeing her reaction of outside.

"I'm just breathing in the fresh air."

"It does stink in that place, doesn't it?"

She was surprised hearing him say that, she had never heard another say anything about the smell before. "Yes, it does and I hate it."

He opened the door for her to get in his car. She watched as he walked around to the other side. She wondered what would happen to her once he was inside of the car. Would he take her somewhere to have her beaten? Would she just be like so many others that come up dead, and never have their remains found. Like the ones that Kevin and Travis had told her about.

"Are you hungry?" he asked looking at her.

She shook her head yes.

"Okay, what sounds good to you?" he looked at her waiting to see what it was that she wanted to eat. Seeing that she said nothing, he thought that maybe she was too afraid to speak. "How does a hamburger sound? Or would you rather have a fish sandwich or something else." He was trying to get her to talk to him.

"A hamburger."

"Okay, we will get you a hamburger, do you want french fries with that and a pop, or an ice cream shake?"

She was wondering if she had him all wrong. He was the only person that have ever asked her what she wanted since she was kidnapped. "I'd like French fries and an ice cream shake please."

"I heard that they call you Cookie, but I'd like to know what your real name is." He looked at her. "Can you tell me your real name?"

"I'm not suppose too."

"Oh, who told you that?"

"Kevin that man that bought me."

"Oh, well you can tell me, I will not let him know that you told me anything." He pulled into the drive through for Burger King. "Can you please trust me; I will never let Kevin know that you told me."

"It's April Davis."

"How old are you April?"

It felt strange for her to hear someone call her April. She liked to hear it; it was the first time since she was picked up from the kidnapper that she's heard it.

He ordered her everything that she wanted. He watched her as he handed the food to her, she ate so fast that he had to ask her to slow down before she was to choke on her food. "How old are you April?" he asked her again.

"I don't know for sure."

"You don't know how old you are?"

"No." she looked at him almost scared of what he might do to her because she couldn't remember her age.

He could see the look of fear in her eyes, and he hurt for her. Just looking at her, he knew that she had been greatly abused by others. "Can you tell me where you live?" he asked.

"I don't know, you picked me up there."

"I'm talking about the home that you had before coming to that one where I picked you up at."

Now Cookie knew that she could never reveal the truth to others. Kevin had given her warnings, that if she did tell anyone what she knows, then they will cut her up in small pieces. "I don't know." She spoke again.

"April, do you have a mom and dad, and a little brother?"

When she heard the man ask her that, she thought that it was a trick. She thought that Kevin had this man pick her up to question her to see if she would tell him the truth about her life. She was so afraid of what might happen to her and her family if she was ever to tell them the truth. "No"

"No, you don't have parents by the name of Joe, and Pat and a little brother by the name of Jimmy?" he looked at her wondering why she would deny her family. "April, I need you to trust me, I am a police officer, I come to bring you back home to your parents. But I first need to know that I am talking with the right child."

She heard what he said, and was still frightened to say anything. "Kevin said that he will cut me up into little pieces and have my family killed if I say anything." She managed to spill out.

"Okay, now I know why you have been afraid to trust me. That's okay, I am taking you to the police station and from there we will call up your folks and let them know that you are safe. How does that sound?"

She began to break with a loud cry, one of which he did not expect to happen. She cried so hard, that her little body shook.

He knew that she was letting out all the fear that she had bottled up for now more then two years of her life. "April, I wanted to tell you that you are nine years old now. Your mother and father had never stopped looking for you. They have done everything that they could to find you. Now that I have found you, your parents will be so happy knowing that their little girl will be back home with them again."

She looked at the man with gentle tears falling down her cheeks. "I'm nine years old now?" she could not believe that she was nine now, because she knew that she was only seven when the kidnapper grabbed her.

"Yes, that is what my paper work tells me. Here we are at the police station." He pulled in to park his car.

"Kevin will hurt me very bad if you don't take me back today. He told me what will happen to me if I decide not to come back." She looked at the police station and felt very scared about going in it.

"April, you never have to be scared of Kevin again. Right now, we have a whole lot of the cops over at the place that I picked you up from. Kevin and all the other men there are being arrested. He cannot hurt you ever again."

She looked at him, but still felt scared what will happen to her if Kevin was to find out that she went to the police station. "But he told me that if I ever talk to the police and say anything about him, he will kill me."

About this time, he knew that April was in need of someone besides himself to talk with her. He was an officer that rescued children from their kidnappers, he was not a therapist. "Let's go in now honey, it is okay, Kevin will never know that you came here with me." He opened her door, and helped her out. The pictures that her parents had given to him, to identify her, looked nothing the same. The girl he had now, was broken and frail. She was thin, and under-weight. He knew that it was the same girl, but he knew that she had been severely abused by the people that held her captive.

April walked into the building with the nice man that gave her good food to eat. She felt scared when seeing so many police officers in there. All she could think of, what would Kevin do to her now. Would he have Travis beat her again, or would he do it himself this time?

"Hello April, my name is officer Mike Spencer. I'd like for you to come with me please."

April was scared of what he wanted from her; she took a hold of the black man's hand tightly. She looked up at him with tears forming in her eyes then dropping down on her clothes. The other officer noticed her reaction, and he knew right away that she was afraid to go alone with him. "Come with us officer Ranks. I believe that she trusts you."

"Yes sir, I believe so." He held her hand and they followed officer Spencer to a back room.

"Now April, I have to say young lady, that I am very happy to see you. Your mom and dad have been looking all over for you for a very long time. Did officer Ranks tell you that you never will go back to that place that he picked you up from?"

She looked at the young officer. "Yes."

"That's good, we have already called up your folks, they are coming here to pick you up. It might take them several hours before they get here. It's a very long drive from your home in Michigan."

"I'll get to see my mom and dad again?" she asked with tears falling again.

"Why don't you take a seat next to officer Ranks. Is there anything that you want to tell me?" he looked at her.

"Anything about the men that held you against your will?"

4

April took a seat next to officer Ranks. She looked at the other officer that was asking questions. "What will happen to all of the other children there?"

He looked at the other officer, then back at April. "We are hoping to return all of them to their families."

"Kevin is an evil man, and so is Travis."

"What else can you tell me about them?"

"They beat me very bad; they made me go days at a time without food."

"Why did they do that to you?"

"Because I didn't do my job very good."

"Your job, what kind of work did you do?"

Tears formed in her eyes just to think about what her job was.

"It's okay to tell us honey, we need to know."

"If I didn't give the men what they wanted when they raped me."

When the officers heard that, it was hard for them to understand the evil of the men that held her and so many others. They knew she must had been being raped, but to hear her say it was hard. "Can you tell me, how often did men come to see you?"

"All day long, when one leaves, another one comes in. when he leaves, then another one comes in."

After they spoke to her about the men that raped her, they had the number a day figured out. There were men coming in raping her anywhere between fifty-sixty times a day. That was hard for then to swallow. The officers sat there looking at each other. Their eyes told everything to each other without speaking a word. The evil that had been done to her and the other children being held there.

"Do you think you might be able to pick out the pictures of the men if I give you a folder to look at?"

"There was a woman too." She softly spoke.

"You seen a woman there too?" surprised a woman was taking place in seeing little children raped and beaten.

"Maybe she might be in the books too, can you look at them please and tell me if you see any of the ones that were at that place that you were at?"

She shook her head yes, then remembered not to shake your head but speak. "Yes."

"Okay, come and sit at this table right over here. I will have you start looking at the first one here." He waited for her to sit down, then he placed the first large book in front of her. "Would you like a drink of pop or water?"

"Yes, please." She opened up the first page. Carefully looking at each picture on the pages. Then she came a crossed one of them. "He is one of them." She pointed to the picture.

"Show me."

She pointed to the picture again. "Here is another one." She spoke putting her finger on the man's face.

The man started to write down the ones that she was pointing out to them. It seemed like she sat for a long time picking out pictures of those that she had seen during the time she was held captive. Some of them were the rapers.

"It's getting late, how would you like to go and lay down for a while, while we wait for your folks to come here?"

Sleep is what she needed, but was afraid that someone would come into where she was at and hurt her. "Kevin will get mad if I don't earn my sleep."

"Kevin." He looked at the other officer, knowing thats what Kevin had done to the small child, was put so much fear into her, that everything she did, she felt like Kevin would be a part of her decision. "Kevin is locked up in jail right now, he will never hurt you again. I have a nice cozy room over here for you, it has a blanket and pillow for you." He could tell by the way she was looking at him, that she was unsure about going into the room, although he could see that she was very tired.

Officer Rank looked at her and took her by the hand. "April, do you trust me?"

"Yes."

"Okay, what I would like for you to do, is go into the room, no one will come in there and hurt you. Its just for you alone, I will be outside of it and make sure that no one will come in. Now why not go and get some sleep, the hour is very late. When your parents get here, I will come in and wake you up."

She looked at him then the other officer. "Okay." She stood up to follow him to a room where a bed was waiting for her.

"Now try not to worry about anything, you are safe with us." He closed the door behind him.

"Poor kid, what those monsters had done to her in two years."

"I bet there are a lot more that she is not saying that's on the inside of her."

"Can you just imagine a little girl like that having men come in and have sex with her fifty-sixty times a day. Wow! The horror she must have gone through."

41

"I can't imagine that happening to anyone let a lone a little girl." The two-officers talked among themselves.

"Has anyone heard any more about the horror house where she was staying at?"

"I'll check on that right now." He called down to the front to see what the word was.

"They have arrested everyone that was at the place. They have brought in all the boys and girls that were being held. They have located some of their parents, and still waiting on the others."

"What about the woman that April told us about? I believe she was called Tina."

"I believe that have her too, they said everyone that was there." Rank said.

"What about the evil men that have been coming into the place to rape these children?"

"We have some undercover men waiting for them to enter there, and once they make a payment to be with a child, they are under arrest at that time. He said they have already got several of them arrested, and brought in."

"That's great, I want them to stay around there until there is no more of them stopping by."

"Yes, they have said that was the plan to do that. What are we suppose to do with all the children that their folks we cannot locate?"

"We will interview each of them, and then we will have to send them over to girls and boy homes, until we can get ahold of a family member."

"I hate to see this happen to them. These kids have been tortured for God only knows for how long, many of them longer than April I'm sure of that. Locked up like a caged animal, then they have to go get locked up again."

"What else can we do; we are the police and not a rescue unit. We help them get free from being raped, and unless we find family to take them in, we have no other choice but place them somewhere."

Rank knew that they could only do so much to help out the children, but the thoughts of family not be able to be found for the ones they brought in, was truly heart breaking. He knew that they had to go somewhere, and just knowing getting them out of sex slavery was far better than where they were at.

April fell to sleep faster then she thought that she would. She hadn't had a peaceful sleep since the day she was kidnapped. It was run with fear of what was going to happen to her next. What she witnessed the other children go through was more than anyone should ever see, let a lone go through it.

After a several hours of her sleeping, officer Rank came in to wake her up. "April, April." He called to the sleepy child.

April opened her eyes, and jumped from sleep. "Yeah."

"Your parents are here for you now." He smiled at her. "Are you ready to go and see them?" he could see the look of fear, even when he mentioned her parents.

"What if they don't want me anymore?" tears ran down her sleepy face.

"Why would you think that way honey? They have drove all night long to come get you." He wiped her tears away. "Let's go and see them, they have waited so long to see you again."

She stood up all the while holding officer Rank's hand. She felt scared of what her parents would think of her now that she had been with so many men. Would they think bad of her, would they blame her?" thoughts ran through her mind.

Walking out in the open room, where her parents stood there waiting to see their little girl, she took a look at them. They looked different from what she remembered. Her mother stood there crying, her father seemed to be much older than she remembered.

"April" her mother called out crying, running to her. "My baby, I have prayed everyday for this moment." She wrapped her arms around her. She knew that it was her daughter, although she looked much different then she was before.

April didn't seem to respond the way her parents thought that she would. She looked at them, in her mind, she had fear that Kevin would kill them now because she was with them again.

Her mother knelt down low to her, and then her father followed. "Baby, I'm so happy to see you again, I have prayed and prayed for this day. I love you sweety and miss you so much." The officer had told them what things she had went through while she was gone for the two years. "Are you okay honey? Are you happy to see us?" her mother questioned her, then looked up at the officer standing close by them. She couldn't understand why April was not saying anything.

"April." Officer Rank spoke.

"Yes." She answered.

"Do you remember when I told you that Kevin or any of those men cannot harm you ever again. They have all been arrested, they are in jail honey. It is okay for you to talk with your mom and dad." He knew what she was thinking, because she had made it known to him beforehand.

"Has Tina been put in jail too?" she asked worried about her coming after her again.

"Yes, even Tina is in jail. You can go home with your parents and know that they will protect you."

April looked at her parents, tears streamed down her little cheeks. "Do you still love me?"

"Oh honey, we love you so much. There is nothing that would take that away from us."

April wrapped her arms around her mother and father. She wept so hard, after all the torture she had endured for two long years she was finally with her family again. She looked at the officer that picked her up from the house of horror. She gave him a smile with a tear-stained face. He knew that she was going to be alright now that she was with her family again.

"Are you ready to go home now honey?" her father asked her.

She shook her head yes, then she remembered that she was not to do that, but she must answer with her voice. Kevin and Tina had given her several warnings about that. "Yes, I am ready to go home." She thought about asking about her brother, but nothing came out. She wondered how he was doing, because her parents had not mentioned him to her.

"Can we take her back home now officer?" the father asked.

"Yes, we will be calling you, when it comes time for going to court." The officer spoke.

On their way home, April wasn't talking, but was sitting in the back seat very quiet. She didn't know what she should say, she was afraid that she might say to much if she started to talk. She knew that Kevin warned her about saying anything about the things that she went through and what she seen other go through. So, she felt she would be safe and keep her family safe if she didn't tell what happened. Even when she spoke with the police officers she never told them everything out of fear of what would happen to her if Kevin found out. Inside there was so much that she wanted to tell her folks, she wanted to tell them how she was beaten and how many men came to her every day and abused her, and stole her innocents from her. How she had gone through more in the last two years then anyone should ever go through, in a whole life time. How she went hungry many times when the evil men that came in her room didn't feel she gave them her best. How she was beaten so badly that it took her weeks to heal. In her mind she wanted to let it all out, but was so scared of what might happen to her again, if Kevin found out.

"How are you doing back there?" Her mother Karen asked her.

April tried to give her a smile, but at the same time, she felt like she couldn't even smile all because she was full of fear.

"April honey, I want you to know that we have cried everyday and prayed asking God to bring us back our little girl."

She listened to her mother talk about praying, but she never knew that they did that before. She never remembered before she was kidnapped that her family talked about God. Was this something new? When did they start talking to God?"

"April, are you hungry?" her father asked her.

She shook her head yes, then spoke it right afterwards. "Yes"

"Okay where would you like to go and eat?" he asked her.

She looked out her window, seeing so many places, so many choices. She had not seen so much since she was kidnapped.

"Can I have a hamburger?"

"Sure, you can, we will stop right up here and use the bathroom and grab a bite to eat." He spoke.

She watched out her window from the back seat to see where her father was going to stop at. She wanted to make sure that it was no where Kevin would see her with them. She watched him pull into a Healthy Burger Place. She thought that must be a new place, because she didn't remember seeing it before. As her father parked his car, she looked all around outside before she got out of the car.

Her mother and father were watching what she was doing, before she stepped out. They both looked at each other, not understanding why she was looking out the window all over before getting out of the car.

"Are you ready to go inside honey?" her mother asked.

"Yes." She stepped out.

They walked into the restaurant to get them something to eat. All the while they watched their daughter become like a complete stranger to them. They knew that she had gone through a very bad time just by the way she was acting, and what the officers had told them. They needed to understand it so they could be of help to her.

Finding a place, a sit down, they wanted her to order anything that she wanted. The waitress came by and handed them their menu's, and asked them what they wanted to drink.

They watched her as she was looking through the menu, it didn't seem like the little girl that they knew before. She didn't even look like the bright-eyed child that they knew. April looked at them, seeing the way they were watching her. She didn't know what she should do, so she weakly smiled at them. "Can I have this hamburger?"

"You can have anything that you want." Her father spoke. "What else do you want besides a hamburger?"

"Can I have a drink too?"

They knew that things had really changed for their little girl, they hurt for whatever she had gone through. "Honey, would you like any French fries too? And what do you want to drink?"

Her father asked her, seeing that she was still holding on the menu.

"Yes please."

After the waitress came and took their order, they wanted to try and get April to open up and talk with them. Because up until this point she had been silent about talking with them.

5

April noticed that her parents were staring at her, she wasn't sure if it was because they hadn't seen her in two years, or because they knew the evil that she had done. None of it was any of her own fault, but she felt like she was to blame those men had done to her what they did.

"I'm sorry we keep looking at you honey. It's just we are so happy to have you back with us again." Her mother spoke. "I want you to know that you can tell your father and I anything that you had gone through. I know that you went through hell on earth honey, and for that we are so sorry."

"Did the police tell you anything about me?" she asked looking at the both of them.

"They did tell us that you were kidnapped by a very evil man, that sold you to another evil man." She didn't want to mention they knew she was sold as a sex slave. She was hoping that her daughter would tell them herself. Tears formed her mother's eyes as she spoke about her daughter being sold.

It didn't take long for April to have soft tears drip down her cheeks. The thoughts of what she had gone through was hell to her. She never knew that there was that kind of evil in the world, until it came to her. One day she was enjoying friends at school, and on her way home from school, to make cookies with her mother and little brother, then her whole life was suddenly changed. "Mom." She spoke then looked at her dad. "I never thought that I was ever going to see you again. I used to lay in bed before the men." She stopped. "I laid there thinking about you, would I ever see you again." Tears dripped down her cheeks again. She looked around the place they were sitting. "Kevin told me that you never wanted me anymore, he told me that you asked them to take me and sell me." Her cries became much more.

Her mother reached her hand out to her, rubbing her arm. "Oh honey, I hope that you never believed them. Those men that did that to you, are going to prison for a very long time. They are just evil people, and your father and I cried and prayed for you every day."

"You never wanted them to take me?" she asked.

"No honey I never did, they told you lies. We love you so much."

"I told them that I didn't believe it, and they told me if I ever mention it to them again, they would cut me up into little pieces and throw my parts all over." She looked at her parents. "I hoped that one day I would be with you again."

Her mother squeezed her hand lightly. "You will never be taken from us again."

"Where is Jimmy at?"

"We let him stay with your aunt Rose while we came here to get you. We knew that it was going to be a long drive, and we also wanted to have this time alone with you."

"Mom." Then she looked at her dad too. "Dad, did you know that I was raped?"

Her parents looked at each other. "I thought that you might have been, but we really don't know what you went through unless you tell us." She tried not to cry hearing what her daughter told her, although she already did know.

"Are you mad at me?"

Her father started to weep, he tried not to, but just hearing his daughter question them if they are mad at her, brought tears to him. "We can never be mad at you; you did nothing wrong." He sobbed some more trying not to allow others to see him cry. He knew he had every right to cry, but he also knew that no one but them understood the tears.

"I hated those men, they hurt me so bad mama, I tried not to let them touch me, but they got mad and beat me."

Her mother and father tried to hold back the tears, so not to draw attention to others. But it chocked them up hearing that from their little girl. "They beat you honey?" her father asked choking back the tears.

She shook her head yes, when tears fell once again run down her cheeks. "I was beaten a lot of time, and they made me go hungry too." She cried as she told of some of the things that she went through.

Her parents hated what she had gone through, all the pain that men had done to her was beyond what they even thought.

"Mom, dad, please never let Kevin come and take me again." She spoke in a quiet whisper.

"Oh honey, Kevin is never going to take you again. He is in jail right now, and after we go to court, he will go to prison I hope forever."

"Court." She looked at her mother, not really knowing what that meant.

"The officers that helped you, told us that we will be needed in court. This is where you will be able to tell your story of what happened to you."

When April heard that, she cried again. "I don't want to tell my story."

Her mom and dad looked at each other. They knew that she really did not understand what it was all about. "We will discuss this later honey. We don't have to worry about that right now." She noticed that the waitress was bringing them their food.

She looked at her mother. "Okay"

They ate their meal, and started back on the long ride home. The father wanted to get his daughter back to their home, where she could see it once again. And help get her mind off of what the men had done to her and hope to get her feeling safe. He loved his little girl deeply, and the thoughts of her being raped by grown men tore him up on the inside. He wanted to scream, knowing what had happened to her. He tried with all his might not to explode in front of her. When he looked at her, he could see the damage of what others had done to her. She looked broken and frail, her eyes looked sunk in, not the bright-eyed beautiful daughter that once was. It was no fault of her own that this has happened. But now it was up to him and his wife, to make sure she gets the proper treatment, and love that she needs to feel whole again. He knew just by the way she acted and looked, that it might take them a very long time to get their little girl back to feeling safe.

"How are you doing honey?" Her mother asked April looking in the back seat of the car.

"I'm okay, I was just thinking that I don't want Kevin to find me."

Her mother looked at her husband, she too knew that April suffered a great deal at the hands of the evil people. She wanted to make her little girl would feel safe, and she was trying everything that she knew. "He won't ever find you or hurt you again honey, he is locked up for a very long time, and he is not coming out." She would remind her again and again.

Her mother could see the way that April was looking at her, almost like an empty stare, like she wasn't seeing anything. It was like April was looking through her and not at her. It made her feel concerned; she didn't know what she ought to do. She looked at her husband. "I think we need to get her set up to see a therapist right away." She whispered low, in hopes that April never heard her.

He looked at her, and speaking in a low voice. "Are you sure that will be necessary?"

"Oh yeah, I know that it will be. I'm sure that your insurance you have at work will cover that."

The two sat in silence, each one thinking and having their own thoughts about April. In the mean time April sat in the back seat staring out the window at every place they drove by and cars next to them. She wanted to see her little brother, it's been two long years since she last seen him or spoke to him. He was not yet in school when she was kidnapped, now that he is five years old, she knew that her parents must have put him into school by now. She wondered if he would even remember her, because she had forgotten what he looks like, after time has passed.

It seemed like they drove for several more hours, with stopping to use the bathroom, and filling the tank up with gas, before finally reaching their home.

Once Micah pulled into the driveway, the hour was already late, and it was dark. April looked at the home, as much as she could see with it being darker outside. She couldn't make it out like she could have had it had been light outside. She sat in the back seat, almost afraid to get out of the car.

"Come on honey, it's okay April, we are home now. "I'm sure that your brother is waiting to see you."

When she heard that her brother would be waiting for her, she stepped her feet out of the car. Standing up, she took her mothers hand to walk with her.

Karen was happy that she decided to take her hand, it made her feel like April was going to be okay, once she reached out to her.

They walked to the house, and Karen opened the door. She waited for April to walk in first. Little Jimmy came running to his mother. He stood there looking at April, like he didn't know her. To April it didn't seem like it was her little brother, he was so much bigger the she remembered. She stood there in the doorway looking at him and how he clinged to their mother.

"Jimmy, do you remember your sister April?" the mother asked, pulling his arms off of her legs.

He looked at his sister. "No."

pril looked at him then her mother. "He looks different then I remember."

"That's probably because he has gotten older now. He is in school now. Come on in honey, does everything look familiar too you?"

April stepped in the house all the way. She stood there looking around her surroundings. "It feels different."

When her mother heard her say that it felt different, she just assumed that she was talking about different from where she had been for the last two years. She never bothered to question if that is what she meant by what she said. "Yes, I'm sure that things are much different?"

April looked at her mother strangely. "Why?" she asked.

"Why what dear?" at this time her mother was very confused why she would ask her why.

"Why is it different now, I don't remember it being like this before."

Karen felt sad that April was not remembering it to be like that before, was she sensing something that Karen was not aware of?" "I'm not sure honey what you mean by that it being different."

"It's nothing, just different then I remembered."

"Do you remember where your bedroom is? That should look the same to you, I haven't changed a thing in there since you been gone."

April looked around her, then towards the stairs. "Will you come with me mommy?"

"Sure, I can come with you." She took her daughters hand and started to walk up the stairs. She wasn't sure why she wanted her to come with her, but she just knew that things had to feel different for her, after her not being home in a long time. She opened the bedroom door for her daughter. "See honey, its just like it was before you were gone."

April stood on the outside of it, she looked at her beautiful bed, and the beautiful blanket that was on it. "Where I slept at there was terrible."

"What was it like for you there?" her mother asked hoping that she would open up a little bit. She knew enough that when someone will hold the pain inside, it lingers for a very long time, but when they talk about it, they could heal so much faster.

Karen didn't expect what was coming after she asked that question. April turned around and wrapped her arms around her mother, bursting into tears. Karen embraced her little girl, knowing that she was broken from the trauma she had gone through. "I'm here honey, and I am so very sorry for what happened to you."

April just stood there crying so hard, her little framed body shook.

"Can we go and sit on your bed? I think that your bed has been very lonely for you." She tried to get her to feel comfortable once again in her own home.

April let go of her mother's waist, but held tightly to her hand. "Mama, those men hurt me so bad." She sat down on her bed and pushed herself up and down a couple of times, then she broke down crying again. "I never thought that I would see my bed again. They had me on an old thing there that stunk really bad." She looked up at her mother with tears falling down. "Mama, did you think about me?"

"Oh, honey every minute of the day, I never slept well since you been gone. I wondered where you were at, and cried for you all the time." She hugged her tightly. "I never want you to ever leave my sight again. I can never lose you again."

"Hold me mama, please never let those men take me away again."

"Never my baby, never again." She cried with her daughter.

"Mama, those men did some bad things to me."

Karen knew that her daughter had been raped, she knew that she had been beaten by men. What she didn't know is the severity of what she had gone through. "I know honey, I know they hurt you. I am so sorry for what happened to you."

"Do you know what they did to me mama?" she cried thinking about what they did to her.

"I know that they beat you up, I know that they raped you honey?"

"They did more then that to me mama."

Karen hated to know the things that she had gone through, but she knew to allow her little girl to share with her all about the trauma she faced by evil people. She hurt to know that her little girl that is only nine years old now had went through the abuse from so many nasty men, raping and beating her since she was seven years old, like she was nothing. "Honey if at any time you want to tell me what they did to you, I am right here to listen for you to tell me okay." She could see that her daughter stopped talking after she said they did more things to her. It was like it hurt her so much to think about it, she couldn't talk about it at this time. Karen was hoping once she got into therapy that it would help her with the trauma.

"Mama does daddy still love me?"

"Oh, my goodness yes, your father loves you so much. He cried for you all the time, and prayed for God to bring you back to us."

"He doesn't say much to me though." She sniffled a little.

"I think that's because he knows that it was men that hurt you the most, and he was not able to do anything about what they did to you. When a man can't fight for his family, they hurt so much inside. But never think for one minute that he does not love you. He is so happy that we have you with us now."

"I feel so tired, can I go to sleep now."

"Sure, honey you can get some sleep, I think we all will be getting sleep. It's very late and your aunt I think is just going to stay the night here, she will want to talk with you tomorrow, will that be alright?"

"Yes mama." She laid down in her bed with all of her clothes on and shoes.

"Oh honey, don't you want to change out of your clothes, and take your shoes off so you can sleep good?"

She sat back up and look around the room. "Okay."

Karen got up and opened up a drawer to get her pajamas. "Here see if this still will fit you. Tomorrow, if your up to it, we will go into town and buy you some knew clothes that fit you good." She looked at the shoes that were much too big for her feet, knowing that they did not belong to her. "We will get you some new shoes too."

April didn't want to undress in front of her mother, she felt ashamed because men had used her. She felt like she was dirty now, and didn't want her mother to see her shame. She held her pajamas close to her, and looked at her mother.

"Oh, do you want me to go out of the room so you can put them on?"

April started to cry. "I'm sorry, I just don't want you to see me naked. I don't look the same anymore." She cried holding tight to her pajamas.

"It's okay, I will go out honey." She didn't know what to say, all she knew is her little girl was broken and she didn't know how to heal her. She knew to love her and make her feel safe, but she didn't know how to treat the trauma she had gone though. There was never a time before now that she wanted her mother to leave the room so she could undress and then dress again. Up until now her and her mother had always had a very close relationship, now everything seems to have gotten lost.

6

The night was one of which Karen and Micah never had expected to happen in their home.

They were sound to sleep, but waken by the screams coming from April's room. The both of them rushed to their daughter's room.

Once opening the bedroom door, they found April sitting on the floor cuddled in the corner of her room. Karen rushed to her side, and tried to help her daughter up off of the floor. "Come on honey." April began to fight as she screamed to the top of her lungs. "No! No leave me alone, I hate you, I hate you." She screamed crying, as she was pushing her mother away from her.

Her father clicked on the light. Without thinking what he was going to say, he yelled out to his daughter. "April stop that now?"

Once she heard her name being yelled and not the name of Cookie, she knew where she was at. She looked at her mother that was next to her on the floor. "Mama, I thought that I was still at Kevin's. Mama, please don't let them take me anymore."

"Oh honey, they can never take you away again. Come on baby, lets get you back in bed." She helped her little girl up off of the floor.

"Mama, can I sleep in your bed with you, I don't want to be alone, I feel scared."

Karen looked at her husband standing by the door.

"You can go into the room with mama honey, I will sleep in your bed tonight." Her father spoke.

Karen held her hand as they walked to her bedroom. "Come on honey, lets get some sleep." As they laid down, Karen started to think about her daughter screaming I hate you. She knew that it was not directed at her, but at the men that raped her. It hurt her to know that her little girl had gone through so much trauma, so much pain and betrayal of grown men and a lady.

She knew that she needed to find help for her daughter to get through all that she had gone through. She felt like she had a troubled mind now.

It hurt her knowing that her daughter would have to go to some kind of a therapist to get healing. As much as she loved her daughter, she knew that she needed more then just a mother's love.

It didn't take April long before she was fast asleep. Karen laid there listening to her daughter breath heavy. She didn't understand why she was breathing so hard. Soon morning was shining through the curtains, and Karen knew that she needed to get up, make some breakfast for her son and husband.

Walking to the kitchen, she seen her husband had already started the coffee. "Good morning." He spoke looking at his wife.

"Morning honey." She gave a slight grin.

"Did you manage to go back to sleep?" he asked.

"Yes, I did, how about you?"

"It took me awhile, but after a little while, I did fall back to sleep. I'm a little worried about April."

"Me too." She confessed.

"What are we going to do?"

"I'm going to make sure that she gets good help from a therapist."

"Honey, look for the best. I know that she has been severely hurt, all though I don't know all that you know. I know you enough by now, that you haven't told me everything that you know. You are trying to spare my feelings."

"I do know you, and I don't want you hurting more then you already are. What good does it do for the both of us to carry this. You have work to do on the outside of the home, as for me, I can be with her and help her. I hope that you don't mind honey, but I know you as her daddy, this would tear you apart."

Micah listened as she explained to him why she was withholding some things from him. He just knotted his head, in saying that he understood her reasoning. "I'll take our son to school today, that way you can stay here with her."

"Oh, thank you honey." She was happy that he offered to take their son to the school. Ever since April had been kidnapped, and Jimmy started school, they have taken him to the school and also picked him up. They never wanted to take a chance that he too would come up missing.

She went about her house work after her husband and son left for the day. She allowed April to sleep as long as she felt like she needed too. She knew that April told her she never slept well the whole time she was at that place being held against her will. It made her spine shiver when she thought about April telling her that every night, as she tried to sleep, men would come into her room and rape her, or beat her, just because they were big and could hurt her any time they wanted too.

She stopped cleaning, and sat down in the living room, and started to cry a deep cry for the pain she knew that her little girl had gone through. It hurt her so much to know there was nothing she could do to save her. She wept uncontrollably, until she felt a light tap on her shoulders. She looked up, thinking that it was April, but it was her sister Rose, awaken by hearing her cries. "I'm sorry to have waken you up."

"No, no never be sorry for that, you have every right to cry about what your child has been through. I heard you talking with Micah last night after the children were in bed. Karen it's such a terrible thing that a bright little girl has gone through this, and then to think about all the others out there going through such things. Man's heart has turned so evil to harm God's little children as they do."

"I need to find a good therapist for her, she screamed in the middle of the night, and wanted to sleep next to me. She thought that she was back there again getting hurt."

"So, what did you do?"

"Micah slept in her bed, and she did with me."

"Oh, honey, I don't know how long that can happen. Is that what is best for you and Micah?" Rose looked at her with questioning eyes.

"We are her parents; we need to make her feel safe for as long as she needs to feel that. She was taken from us for two long years. She has been through hell on earth, men raping her up to fifty-sixty times a day." She looked at her sister, and seeing Rose's eyes get big like saucers.

"Fifty-sixty times a day she was being raped?" she just couldn't believe a little girl could even live through such wickedness. "I had no idea, that poor child, no wonder she would wake up screaming, I would too and I'm an adult."

"This is why, I need to find someone that has dealt with others that's been through this. I need to have someone that knows how to handle this type of issue. I may be her mother, and I love her so much, but I just don't know what I can do for her besides love her and be there for her."

"What does Micah say about what happened to her? I know how a father can be about their daughters."

"He knows that she has been raped, but how much, I have not told him. I know how he is, and I don't need him walking around like a mad man. He needs to focus on working and caring for his family. If he knew what she all went through, he could not keep good focus, he would be thinking to much about what happened to her. So please never tell him anything that you find out, leave that up to me and April to tell him."

"My lips are sealed, but as far as a good therapist, I know just the person. She is a woman that has delt with girls from all walks of life. She is a Christian and understands their needs."

"Really, who is it then."

"Her name is Ellie Walker from our church."

"You're kidding me, Ellie?"

"Yes Ellie, she has been doing this for over twenty years, she is the one that you want to call and talk with her about April."

"I'm going to call right now before April comes down stairs." She looked up Ellies name in the phone book. She knew her from the church and knew that both she and her husband are good people. "Hello, Ellie, this is Karen Davis."

"Oh, hello, how are you doing?" she asked.

"Ellie, I'm trying to find someone that can help my daughter April. Rose told me that you are a therapist."

"Yes, I am, I heard about your daughter, all though I have not heard any details about her. Can you tell me what is going on with her and how old is she?"

"She is nine years old now, but when she was seven, she was kidnapped walking home from the school bus stop. She was kidnapped and sold into sex trafficking."

"Oh, dear Jesus. I did not know that. Continue please, what is it like for her?"

"We just got her back after two years, and she has told me that fifty-sixty times a day men would rape her. Is that really possible? I mean she is only nine years old, can she be just imagining that it happened like that?"

"Oh, no she would not be imagining it, that is very true. I have helped a few cases such like this one, and they have said the very same thing. These wicked men make millions of dollars selling these children to other men for sex. Has she ever mentioned to you about being beat up by any of the men, or having to go without food for days at a time?"

Karen had tears come down her cheeks, up until this time, she really wanted to believe that April only imagined having gone through so much, although she did know she had gone through hell on earth, but now after hearing from Ellie, she knew what April told her was all true. "Yes, she told me all of that had happened to her."

"Karen, your daughter will need to start right away of getting help. When would you like to start bringing her in, I'm assuming that is why you called me."

"Yes, it is, I know that she needs more help than I can give to her."

"Okay, when is the best time to start for you?" Ellie asked.

"Here the things, I'm wondering if you accept my husband's insurance."

They talked about who their insurance was through and found out that Ellie did accept it. "Great, then we can start whenever you have an opening."

"Let's see." She looked through her schedule. "I have an opening on Wednesday at ten o'clock. Does that work for you?"

"Yes, now how long do you think something like this is needed for?"

"I can never say, some girls never heal from trauma, others seem to bounce back fairly well. All we can do is keep loving her during the stressful times, and keep bringing her here twice a week, until she seems to be able to handle life without it."

"Twice a week?" she asked.

"Yes, we will give that a try in hopes that it will help her more. I will see her every Wednesday and Friday. Same time at ten for each session."

"Okay, I will see you then, and thank you so very much."

After she hung up the phone, she looked at her sister. "Well, she is going to start seeing April twice a week, starting on Wednesday. I really hope and pray that this will help her heal from all the trauma she had gone through."

"Me too, it's a very evil place in one's mind when they feel the need to use little children to give them what a grown up can do."

"I really don't believe that it's about sex at all."

"Why would you say that, when that is what they are doing, having sex with the children."

"Yes, I understand that, but I truly believe its all about stealing the children's innocence. The devil hates the children I think more then anyone, because they are little and cannot defend their self. He knows that if he can destroy the children's future, then he has wiped-out a generation of children. He is after our children any way he can get to them, rather by selling them, raping them, cutting them up in pieces like abortion, or human sacrifice. Even when it comes time to have our little small boys, getting their genitals cut off and made to be little girls. Its all about stealing the children in some kind of format."

Rose listened to her sister talk so passionately about the children. She knew that she had always loved little children even before her daughter April was kidnapped, but this has just opened her eyes more to see what is going on with the children. "Yes, I understand, you must do whatever you and Micah feel that you can to help her. I really believe that going to see Ellie is going to help her out a lot."

As the two were talking, April came down the stairs. She stood at the bottom looking at her aunt. "Hi Auntie." She spoke in a soft voice.

"Hello honey, did you get a good sleep?" she didn't know why she asked that question, after-all Karen had told her what took place.

"After I went to sleep with mama, I did." She looked at her mother. "Is daddy mad at me for coming into your room?"

"No honey, not at all. Why would he be upset with you. You're our daughter and have not been home in a long time. You can sleep there until you feel that you can go back in your room once again." She smiled at her holding out her arms for her. She just wanted to hug her and let her know she was loved.

April walked over to her mother and allowed her to be hugged by her.

"I love you so much April and so does your father. He told me just today, that its okay for him to sleep in your room as long as you need him too. That way you can sleep in my room, and feel better okay."

"Okay mama."

The three talked for a while, until it was time for the aunt to leave to go back to her own home. "Call me anytime you want to talk." She told her sister and April.

"Okay we will do that."

Karen made breakfast for April, hoping that she would eat everything that she made. "Look honey, I made you your favorite kind of pancakes. Just like you like them." She slid the plate over to her, and she sat down to eat a couple with her.

She watched as April stared at her plate of pancakes before taking a bite.

"Honey, is there something wrong?" she questioned.

"No, I was just thinking about how I never thought that I would eat these again." She looked at her mother, soft tears formed her eyes. "I never knew that I would come home again. I never knew how much I would miss being home, until I was gone." She started to weep with knowing she was home now, and safe.

Karen teared up listening to her daughter talk what was on her heart. She rubbed her daughters back with her hand. "You made it honey, and you never will have to go back to that wicked place again."

"Mama."

"Yes baby."

"Kevin told me that I needed to talk with a girl there that was across the hallway from me."

"Talk to her about what?"

"He told me that I needed to tell her what they did there, and if she gave them a hard time, she would be beaten, and go without food."

Karen just hated to hear the evil that was done to her daughter, but she knew that she needed to talk about what she went through.

"When I told her what they do, she started to cry mama. I told her that there was going to be a lot of pain that comes to her." Tears fell down her cheeks. "I heard when the men came in to see her. She was screaming and crying when she was being raped. I could hear her pain; I knew what they were doing to her. Mama, she died."

"Oh, my gosh, she died?"

"I don't know if they killed her or if she killed herself. I tried to kill myself."

Karen had a hard time hearing that come from her daughter. "You tried to kill yourself?"

"The pain is so bad mama, all those big men coming into your room and hurting you over and over again. I hated my life, and I never thought that

I would see you again. They told me you hated me and that you gave me away to them to sell."

She wrapped her arms around her daughter, she broke down in a hard cry along side her daughter. "Honey, if you would have died, I would never have known what happened to you. I'm so sorry for what you went through, and how evil all of them people were to you and all the children there. But I am so happy, that you never died. Every day that you been gone, I fought to stay alive. I wanted to die so many times; I had a hard time moving on with life. Had it not been for your brother and father, I would have died."

"I'm glad that you never died mama."

"I'm glad that you never did either honey, now we have each other, and we can heal together."

"Okay." She smiled a weak smile at her mother. She looked at her pancakes again, and started to eat them. "These are so good mama, I never had them there." She ate until her plate was clean of every piece of pancake.

7

April had been going to therapy for two weeks now. There was a small part that she seemed to be doing better at night time, but it never lasted long. She still would wake up screaming and crying in otter fear of what was happening to her. After her mother would wake her up and reassure her that she was no longer being raped, she would fall back to sleep.

"Mama, I'm sorry about waking you up again."

"It's okay honey, I understand. Your getting better honey, you're not screaming as much as you were before, so I know that Ellie is able to help."

"I really like Mrs. Walker; she is very nice and I like the way she talks to me."

Karen was pleased in hearing that April liked her therapist. She knew if she liked her then she would be more able to receive from her the help that was offered. "That's great honey. I know that she likes you too."

"Mama, how long do you think that I will have to go and see Mrs. Walker?"

"I'm not sure honey, I guess until we see that you are able to sleep in your own bed again, and not have terrible nightmares of you still being at that place."

She looked sad. "I hate those nightmares mama, it always shows me what happened to me when I was there."

"I know honey, but I also know that God is going to see you get better, where the nightmares will forever go away."

She smiled at the sound of that. "Mama, do you think that we can make cookies today?" once she mentioned the word cookies, the look on her face was no longer happy.

"Sure, we can, I know that we used to like doing that before." She noticed the unhappy look on her face. "What's wrong honey, why do you look so sad now?"

"I don't want to make then now."

"Why not dear?" she couldn't understand what changed her mind so quickly. Could it have been the thought of something she used to do before.

"I don't want to talk about it." She walked away and went to sit down in a chair in the living room.

Karen knew that there was something she did not want to talk about. She wasn't sure if she should press the issue or let it go. This was one of those times she really wished she knew what was the right thing to do. She looked at April sitting all alone in the front room, seeing the look of sadness and despair written all over her. The pain was just too much for her to stand there and watch her. She needed to reach out to her as a concerned loving mother. "April, honey can you talk with me please. I want to help you honey, but when you clam up like this, I don't know what I ought to do. Please baby talk to mama, tell me what changed your mind about us baking some cookies." She pleaded with her.

April looked at her mother, tears fell to the floor. "Did I tell you that when that mean man picked me up and took me to Kevin, he called me Cookie, he told me that was going to be my new name. I was never called April the whole time I was there, I was only called Cookie." She wept to where her small frame body shook with tears.

At least now Karen understood where she was coming from, and she could not blame her at all. So, it was up to her to make a new name up for baking cookies, to where April could feel excited to bake them again, without the reminder of the pain of the name cookie.

"How about us calling them a new name. We don't ever have to use that old name again, but we can still enjoy baking again." She tried to get April into the spirit of baking with her again.

"Okay, what can we call them?"

"What if we call them baking happy rounds. What do you think?"

"Happy rounds?"

"Yeah, because they are round, and it makes us happy to bake them."

"Okay mama, we can call them happy rounds." She put a smile on her face, knowing that she could enjoy baking again with her mother.

The two walked back into the kitchen and got out everything that was needed to bake some happy rounds. They talked as much as they could, although there were some small issues at times to where April would cry about certain thing's she remembered happened to her.

Karen allowed her to feel what she was at the time she spoke about them. She would just hug her and encourage her that things were getting better.

In the middle of them cooking, the phone rang. "Hello" spoke Karen when she answered the phone.

"Hello is this Mrs. Davis?"

"Yes, this is she."

"This is Sargent Whitmore; I spoke with you and your husband when you came to our station to pick up your daughter April."

"Yes, I remember." She was wondering why he was calling them now.

"The men that had your daughter held at the place for two years are going to court. We will need your daughter to come and testify in court against them."

"I remember that you had mentioned that to my husband and myself. I just don't know how easy that will be."

"Mrs. Davis, your daughter picked these men out in our books. She knows who they are and what they did. We want to make sure these people go away for many years. If she does not come to court, then there is a chance they all can walk. Now I know after the hell she had gone through with them; we don't not want that to happen again to another child."

Karen was listening to him talk, as she was watching April with the happy rounds. She hated the thoughts that she would have to face those men again. After all the evil they did to her, she knew that it was going to be hard for her to do that. "I will speak with my husband when he comes home tonight, and also speak to April about it."

"Mrs. Davis, I understand you feeling hesitant about this, I would feel the same way if it were my child. But I hate to have them slip through our court system and be released because a lack of evidence."

Karen knew he was right; she didn't want that to happen either. She just wished that there was another way, without it involving April to face to see them again. She knew that she was already going through a rough time. "I understand what you are saying, I will call you back tomorrow. When did you say court is?"

He told her again when April would be needed in court. "Please call me at your earliest convenient tomorrow."

"Yes, I will. Thank, you for calling me about this matter." After she hung up the phone, she tried to act like it was just a normal call. She walked back over to April cutting out some of the happy rounds. "How are you doing here?" she said looking at how many she had already cut out.

"Mama, who was that on the phone?"

"Oh, just a man honey." She hated to tell her what it was really about.

April might have only been nine years old, but she had gone through so much in the last two years of her life, she was forced to grow up way before her time. She had seen and heard things that she should have never seen or had gone through in a life time. She was wiser than what others seen her as. "Mama, I heard you mention court."

Karen never remembered mentioning court to the man, but now she knew that she had to be honest with her daughter. "April, that phone call was from Sargant Whitmore. Do you remember him?"

She shrugged her shoulders. "I don't know."

"He was there when your father and I came there to pick you up."

"I remember the black man, he was officer Ranks, and then officer Spencer."

"Yes, them too. But there was a Sargant Whitmore, we spoke with him before we seen you."

"Okay, I don't think I talked to him though. What did he want mama?"

"I don't know if you remember or not, but there was talk about one day, you may be called to come to the court house and talk in court against the people that did this to you and all of the other children that were there."

"No, mama, I don't want to go to court." She said that then she looked at her mother. "Will I have to see them there?"

"Honey, Sargant Whitmore explained to me, if you did not come and tell the court what these evil men had done to you and the other children, then the court might have to let them go free."

April froze in place, she looked at her mother with so much fear in her eyes, that it scared Karen to see it. "You said that I will never have to see them again."

"April, what I told you honey, is that you will never have to go with them again. I always knew that there was a possibility that you might have to go to court. April, I don't like this either, and I don't want to force you to go, but if you don't go and tell what you know, they may get out of jail. Then they will be free to do the same rotten things to other little boys and girls again."

April hated the thought of having to see them again, but she hated the thoughts of them being let out of jail to hurt others even more. "I never want them to get out, I will go to court and tell the judge what I know."

Her mother was in unbelief of how grown up her little girl spoke at the time. She knew that this was not an easy choice for her to make, she knew for her to see those men again would be very hard. But yet she spoke like a big girl and decided to go to court and speak out against the evil works of what they men and Tina had done.

"I'm so proud of you honey, I know that was not an easy choice to make. I want you to remember this, once this court stuff is all over with, you will never have to see them again."

"Good."

"So how are our happy rounds doing?" she spoke trying to change the subject and bring a happy moment to come in.

"I have this pan all filled, it needs to go into the oven now."

She spoke carrying the pan to the oven.

Karen pulled the door down so she could put the pan in. "Now be careful so you don't touch the hot wires."

"I'll be careful mama. I remember when you taught me that a long time ago."

"You do huh, I'm glad to know you remembered it."

They finished up their baking of their happy rounds. After the batches were all done, they cleaned up the mess in the kitchen and sat down to eat some of their fresh baking.

When it came time for the school to be letting out, April went for a drive with her mother to go and pick Jimmy up at the school. "I miss my friends mama." She spoke looking at the school, while watching Jimmy walking towards them.

Right when they were sitting on the outside of the school, they noticed a man walk up and pick up a little girl walking towards the bus. The girl started to scream and kick. "Hurry Jimmy, get in the car." April call 911 tell them we are at the school and to get here fast. Karen jumped out of the car and ran to the man that was carrying off the little girl. She began to fight the man by kicking him and screaming at him to let the child go. She was yelling so loud, that it drew the attention of others that were nearby. Some stood not knowing what was going on, then there were some women came to help her out. Once fighting the man, the women folks were able to get the little girl free from the man. Karen watched as he ran to a dark older car. He took off in it at a high rated speed. Then she went to the little girl again. "Did you know who that man was honey?"

"No." she spoke.

"What bus were you going too." She asked the child, then she thought that maybe she should wait until the police arrived there. "Thank all of you ladies for coming to help me get this child away from that man.

She watched as the police pulled into the parking lot, she held on to the little girl's hand and walked over to the policeman. "Hello, I had my daughter call you when I see a man grab ahold of this little girl, and try to kidnap her."

The officer pulled out a notepad and started to write. He asked for Karen's name and the child's. "How did you know that the man was going to kidnap her?"

Karen told him what she witnessed and how all the other women joined in to help get the girl free from him. And how she watched him drive off in a dark older car. They stood around talking for a while all the while the little girl's parents were called up and asked to come to the school to pick her up.

Once the mother arrived there at the school, and she heard about what happened, she started to cry at the thoughts that her little girl could have been taken away from them that very day, right off of the school grounds. "Thank you so much for fighting that man to get my daughter away from him. I just don't know what I would have ever done without her."

"My daughter was kidnapped two years ago, and sold into sex trafficking, I just got her back about three weeks ago. I cannot stand to see what these evil people are doing to our children." She never planned on telling her story about what happened to her daughter, but it just came out of her mouth in the heat of the moment.

"Thank you so much, I don't know how I can ever repay you."

"There is no need for that, I'm just so thankful that I was here at the right time to see this happen, so I could do something to help. All of these women also helped me get her free. She pointed out to the other three that came to help her once they heard her screams.

Once going back home, April was in tears too at what she seen happening to another child younger than herself. "Mama, I'm so happy we were here to pick Jimmy up. If we weren't here, that man would have taken that girl and did some very evil things to her."

"Yes honey, I am sure that he would have." She was thanking God at this time that she was able to get the little girl away from the man.

After arriving home, Karen started to give Jimmy a happy round. "Here Jimmy here is a happy round for you." She handed him one. She was trying to not show her children just how frightened she really was by what happened at the school.

"Why are you calling it a happy round mama?"

"Because your sister and I wanted to call it something that makes us happy. They make us happy to bake them and they are round." She looked at him, giving him a smile.

"Okay mama, they taste good." He said after taking a big bite of it.

"How was school today, Jimmy?" asked April.

"It was boring, I wanted to come home."

"Well, you are home now." Spoke his mama. "You can go and play in the back yard if you want while I start cooking the supper."

"Okay mama."

Karen could trust him being safe in the back yard. After April was taken, her and her husband put in an eight-foot-tall wooden fence all around the large back yard. Not only did they put in a large fence, but they also had a play station built for him back there. It had the wall climbing, a slide, two swings, and a hooked-on bridge. Then there was a trampoline in the back yard and a pool. They wanted everything that was needed to keep him occupied so he could spend hours in the back yard with friends, or by himself without getting board. On all the sides of the fence, was a three-foot wooden brace that came out from the top of it. So if anyone tried to come over the fence, they could not. They also had four cameras in the back yard in every corner of the fence. She felt he was safe without her having to check on him every few minutes.

"Mama, I really like what you and daddy did with the back yard. I don't think anyone can go back there to take him."

"Nope there will be no uninvited guest going back there. April after you were taken, it devasted your dad and I. We didn't know what we were going to do for the longest time. We were so scared to let Jimmy out of our sight, we still won't let him go over to a friend's house and play. So, we had to come up with something that will make him feel safe and it not bother him so much when he can't go to his friends."

"But what about him getting out to see others and do things?" she asked.

8

"Your father has taken him to baseball games, and he played on a team last year. But I was there for every practice and game that he had. Also, we have been invited by aunt Rose and uncle Rob to go camping with them, and we did that for a week. Jimmy took his bike and rode around with your cousins. He was very safe there and was watched all the time. After that time, we bought our own camper."

"That is good mama. Does he have any of his friends that come here?"

"They did all the time until you came back home."

"Why not now mama?"

"We didn't want to make you feel overwhelmed. I wanted to give you time to be home again, and get used to things, before others would come around."

"I think it would be nice if Jimmy could have some friends come over. I would go outside with them and watch them."

Karen looked at her daughter. "April, you know honey, little boys can get very loud, and rowdy."

"Mama, it will be nothing like when I was at Kevin's. These boys will be screaming while playing and having fun. They won't be screaming because they are being raped and beaten."

Karen choked back some tears when she heard her daughter speak so much like a grown child and not a little nine-year-old. Sometimes what came out of her daughter's mouth shocked her. It was amazing the heart she felt towards others. "Okay, if you feel like it wouldn't bother you that he has some friends come over, I will let him know that."

"Good, does he go swimming by himself?"

"Sometimes he does, we have life savers out there on the deck. He knows that he is never to go into the swimming pool without one."

"Can I go swimming with Jimmy?"

"Oh, sure you can honey, that is just as much as yours than it is any ones."

"Can I go swimming with him now if he wants too."

"You sure can, go outside and asked him if he wants too."

It didn't take April long before she was quickly out the door, and running to where Jimmy was at playing in a sand box with some trucks. "Jimmy, do you want to go swimming with me"

Jimmy was surprised that she was asking him that, she had been home for three weeks and never asked to go swimming. "Did mama say we can?"

"Yes, she did, so do you want too?"

"Yes, I do."

"Okay we need to get in our swim clothes." he spoke running towards the house to change into his swim shorts.

Karen watched the two go to the pool once they changed their clothes. She was so happy that April wanted to go swimming with her little brother. She continued to cook supper all the while looking out the sliding glass doors into the back yard. She watched as Jimmy and April put on life savers before going into the pool. Standing at the glass doors watching them, she started to laugh when she seen them throwing water at each other. They were laughing and having a good time. Karen began to cry to see her daughter happy for the first time. She loved watching both of her children enjoy playing in the pool together. After an hour went by, she knew that their father was going to be home anytime from work. She needed to have the children come in the house and change out of their wet clothes, so they could eat supper with her and her husband. "Kids, hey kids, we need to have you come in now. Your dad will be home and he will be ready to eat."

She closed the door after yelling for them. She watched as they took off their life jackets, and started to walk towards the house.

"That was so much fun mama. Do you think that Jimmy and I can go swimming again?"

"Sure, you can go swimming, its just right now is about time for us to eat as a family. I know how much your dad loves for all of us to eat together."

"I know that he does, now that I'm back home huh mama." She spoke so sweetly.

"Yes honey, he loves to see you and know that you are still here with us and doing good."

"Me too." She spoke.

April helped her mom set the table setting, and place the food onto the table. She loved to help her mother, it almost seemed like she felt normal when she stayed busy doing something. She didn't have time to think about what she had gone through or what the evil men looked like. "Daddys home now." She spoke seeing that her father pulled into the driveway.

"Oh good, do you want to call for Jimmy to come down stair now. Tell him that we will be eating soon." Karen asked April seeing that she was liking to be doing things. She seemed to be a peace when she was busy, and anything that would keep her at peace Karen was all for.

After the table was all set and everyone was sitting, they held hands and Micah prayed over the meal.

"Amen." Each one said when the prayer was finished.

Micah focused his attention on April. "Mom tells me that you went swimming today."

"Yes, I did with Jimmy." She smiled, when ever she spoke to her dad, she felt shy. She didn't see or talk with him very much.

"I can tell by the smile that you must have enjoyed yourself."

"Yes, I did. I want to do it again, and mama said that would be alright if I did." She spoke as if she needed his approval on doing so.

"Absolutely, I want to see you swim as much as you like. Also, Jimmy will love being able to swim with you too."

That made her happy knowing that he didn't mind she go swimming.

"I was thinking, how about the family go away for the weekend. Maybe do a little bit of camping?" he looked at his wife.

"Are you sure that we should be doing that now?" she worried about her children being alone to play, unless she and her husband were with them the whole time.

"I think so, why not. It's a quiet place and the children will be able to have so much fun."

"Which place is it that you are talking about?"

"Yellow Stone Park, there is so much to keep the children busy, and us too."

He talked her into going away for the weekend. She didn't really feel like it was time for doing that, but she could tell that her husband was very adamant about going.

In days ahead she prepared the things that they would be taking on their weekend vacation. She wanted to make sure that enough food was packed in the camper, along with the clothes they would need. Bug spray and lights to hang on the outside of the camper. She knew that after work come Friday when her husband would be coming home, he would want to leave right away for their weekend of camping.

The more she thought about the place they were going, was all the more she felt an excitement to show April the place they started to go about a year ago. It was a stress relief for her and her husband, a nice get away from always thinking about their little girl being gone.

At the time it was Rose and her husband that first started them to want to start camping, after the first time, they felt it was good for them to have a get away once in a while. A time for something besides always being at the home to think about their daughter they had no idea where she was or if she was still alive. Each time they walked past her bedroom, it was like a knife being thrusted into them. There were times it took everything they had to stay awake and keep living. Karen and her husband at times just wanted to lay down and die, it felt like they could not continue on another day. But then there was Jimmy their son, they were forced to remain alive for him. To none his fault, but he was only three years old, he needed his mom and dad both to love and care for him. Out of his need, they found themselves still living, and continuing on in life.

Although things seemed to get easier to do, repeating the same actions every day, their daughter was still always in their heart and mind.

One day Karen met a woman on the streets that had dropped her bag of groceries. Karen knelt down to help her pick up her food, when the lady began to talk to her about Jesus, and the church that she goes too. She invited Karen and her family to come out on Sunday and see how they liked it. Karen never was into going to church, both her and her husband had never gone their whole married life. She decided to try something out of desperation that she had never done before.

After telling her husband that she wanted to go to church and she would like for him and Jimmy to come with her, he too knew that they needed something more than what they had.

Ever since that very first time going to church, they have gone every week, even most mid-week services.

"April." Karen spoke.

"Yes mama."

"Have you been liking it since you been going to church with us?"

"I like it mom, I like my Sunday school teacher too."

"I know that I ask you before, but you weren't sure at the time. But I noticed last Sunday you seemed to enjoy it more."

"I like it mom and I make me a friend there too. Her name is Cameron."

"Oh, honey that is great."

"We sit next to each other in class. And we sing together too."

Karen chuckled knowing that April was opening up a little more each day. She was happy to see the good days come where she was bright eyes and on the positive note. Then the days where she was still having a hard time to coup, those were the days that Karen had to take a deep breath and pray through it.

Friday came soon enough. "April are you ready to go to your therapy?"

"Yes mama."

"Okay, after your dad gets home tonight, we will be leaving for the camping trip."

"Will I have fun mama?"

"I think that you will, you like to swim, and they have several ways you can go swimming there. You will enjoy yourself. Let's get going honey we don't want to be late to see Mrs. Walker.

April put her shoes on and walked to the door. She liked going to see Mrs. Walker, she always seemed to feel better after talking with her for an hour each time she went there.

In some ways Karen was hoping that April would continue to see Ellie, it seemed to help April in so many ways. It was like she would open herself up more to talk about the things that she had gone through, and it became easier for her during the night to sleep better.

Karen would do anything to help her children out, and she was so thankful to finally have her daughter home with them once again. But she missed sleeping next to her husband, they were still a young couple, and they wanted to be able to show their love to each other. She was hoping that April would willingly say that she felt like she could sleep in her own bed again. Karen was thinking since they were going camping, that she was going to lay down the sleeping arrangements in love but with the authority she had as a mother, and maybe this will give April the want to be able to start sleeping in her own bed at night.

They had bunkbeds, for the children and then a big bed for mom and dad in the back end of the camper. She knew that her husband was not going to want to sleep on the bunkbed, so she was going to let April know that it's for the children only. She smiled at the thought of how she was planning on telling her the way that it was going to be. Waiting in the waiting room for April to be done for the day with Ellie, she had many plans running there her thoughts.

She knew that she was not going to allow the children to run off and play on their own. There was no way that going to happen even if they felt like that wanted to do that. There were thousands of people at those kinds of parks, and it was impossible to know everyone that came through there. So, she or her husband would have to be with them at all times.

She remembered the first time that her sister Rose had invited them to go camping. She hated the thoughts of doing that, all she could think about what if that is the time that April would come back home. But once she was convinced into going, she loved the get away time. It seemed to help her to get away from the house, and having to walk past April's room all the time.

April walked out of Ellies office, she smiled at her mom. "I'm ready to go now mama."

"Great, how did it go today?"

"I cried a lot."

Karen understood that, she knew that Ellie would get April to talk about the hurt and pain that she had gone through. She needed much healing deep down inside of her. But also, she needed to find it in her heart to forgive everyone that had violated her. Whenever Karen talked with her daughter about forgiveness, it was like April would clam up and stop talking. She could understand that feeling, because even she as an adult that hasn't gone through that type of pain and rejection had a hard time forgiving the men that had raped her daughter and beat her up.

She would just hope and pray that the Lord would continue to show April his love, so she in time could allow herself to forgive those men that hurt her, and stole her innocents.

"Well, we will be leaving for our camping trip today. Are you all pack and ready?" Karen asked April.

"I think so mama. Did you say for me to bring a bathing suit?"

"Yes, I did, there are several different places where you can either go swimming or slide down a huge slide and it's a wet slide."

"Will there be a lot of men there?"

Karen heard in her daughters voice the concern, it bothered her knowing that she felt fear. "Honey men are a part of the family's lives. Just like your daddy is of ours. There will be many men that come there, but I promise you, not one of them will touch you. Either your dad or I will be there with you the whole time."

"But what about Jimmy, they hurt little boys too."

"Your dad and I will be with the both of you the whole time. We will not let you go anywhere on your own."

April never said anything else at the time, she remained quiet. Karen wasn't sure if that was a good thing or not. She quietly prayed. *"Oh, Lord, you know the stress and pain all of this has caused our family. I am asking for you to give April peace, and her father and I during this time. Help her to know that she will be protected and no harm will happen to her again, in Jesus' name I pray, amen."* "April, its going to be okay, nothing will happen to you or Jimmy okay." She was hoping that April would say something just to let her know that she was okay.

"Okay April." She said again.

"Okay mama."

After Karen reached home, both she and April finished packing the camper. They wanted everything all packed and ready before Micah came home from work.

9

Micah arrived home, he was excited to begin the weekend away from home. The camper was all packed with everything that was needed for their fun time away.

"Is everyone all ready to head out?" Micah asked.

"We are all ready, April and I spent the day packing and making sure not to forget anything."

"Great, then are we all ready to go? We can eat there."

"Yep, we are ready, just hook the camper up and we can go." Karen said.

Micah heard what his wife had said and he knew that when she said everything was all packed up, then he could trust that it was. "Okay I will go and do that right now, kids you might as well get into the truck so after the camper is hooked up, we can leave."

April and Jimmy walked outside to get in the truck like their dad had asked them to do.

Micah watched them get into the truck, then he focused his attention to his wife. "Honey, I don't know if you thought about this or not, but I don't think that I will be able to sleep in a bunkbed."

She chuckled. "You won't have too, that is already taken care of, you and I will be together in the back bed. April will take a bunkbed."

"Really! That is great news, have you already told her?"

"Yes, I did, I showed her how it is not fit for a large person such as yourself, but it's meant for children. I assured her that she will be safe and no one will get her."

"Thank you, baby, I wanted so much for us to be able to lay next to each other again."

"Micah is this why you wanted us to go on a vacation so much?"

"I did have the thoughts, that I would really like to come back into our bedroom at night. I miss my wife, and want to be with her not held up in our daughter's bedroom. I'm hoping that after this weekend, April will start to want to go back to her own room."

"Trust me I understand that, and also, I miss our alone time, where we lay there and just talk. There are things that have happened in this past week I haven't even talked to you about."

"Let's go honey, the kids are waiting for us, and its hot out there. I want you to tell me everything that you haven't been able to talk with me about."

"Okay, let me grab my purse, and then I am ready."

They made sure the door was all locked up, and closed tight. Once on the road for their two-hour drive, Karen could see the kids in the back watching a movie on their iPad, so she knew it would be a good time to talk with her husband. Both kids had their headphones on and would not be able to hear her talk.

"Honey, I never told you about the kidnapping I witnessed the other day at the school." She spoke looking at him.

"What? A kidnapping."

"It was one that almost happened. April and I were there to pick up Jimmy, when I see this man grab ahold of a little girl, and she began to scream and kick, something came over me. I went into a rage like a mad woman. I told April to call 911, and I ran to help the little girl. I began to fight that monster of a man, I too began to scream so loud, that others took notice. There were three other women that came and joined in grabbing the hands of that man, I started kicking him and biting him, he finally let go of the girl. He took off running to his car and drove off."

"Karen, are you freaking kidding me? All of that happened at the school, and you never even mentioned it to me?" he was upset that she failed to tell him about that.

"Honey please, you don't need to get so angry. I didn't want to talk about it in front of the children. It really bothered April to see that happen.

After what she went through, I could tell that she hated to see it almost happen again to another little girl."

"I'll tell you one thing; we are not going to leave our children unattended for one minute. We must keep a close eye on them all the time."

"I already know that, and I had to let April know that too."

"How is she doing in therapy?"

"I think she is getting so much better, haven't you noticed that?"

"Yes, I have, and I am so happy about that. I wasn't sure if it was her going to therapy or what."

"Ellie is wonderful, that is helping April out so much to go and see her. She has come so much future since seeing Ellie. She's talking about things a lot more, and when she does, she's not breaking down crying every five minutes."

"Maybe I will get a chance to really talk with her this weekend. Did you grab any games that we can play together at the camper as a family?"

"Yes, I did. I brought our lights to hang, and our table and fold up chairs. I went shopping and picked up lots of snacks and food for the whole weekend."

"That's great, I'm very excited to be having a break from home and taking a little time for a get-away."

"I know honey, you work so hard to take care of us, and I know you need a good break. I do need to tell you another thing that I had forgotten all about."

Micah looked at her with a frown on his face. "What now."

"We will have to go to court next week."

"Court for what?"

"Sargant Whitmore called the other day, do you remember when we went to go and pick up April, he told us that we will need to bring her to testify against those men?"

He thought about that for a minute. "Yeah, I guess."

"I can see that your unsure, I was at first too when he called. But he made a very good point. April is the one that picked them men out in the criminal books at the jail. She has to go to court and tell them what happened to her and what she seen happen to many others. He told me that if she does not go and tell the truth, then there is a good chance those men will walk free because of lack of evidence."

"Oh my gosh, our baby has to go and see those evil men that had raped her." He was in shock. "I hate that, they arrested those men at the place along with so many other children that were there, why do they need April?"

"I don't know honey, but April said that she wants to go."

"She, said that? Really, she wants to go to court and be able to see those men again?"

"She, told me that she wants to testify against them, she wants the court to know everything that they did so they will get locked up for a very long time and not get out to hurt anyone else again. I don't want to take that right away from her." She watched her husband's reaction when she talked to him. She could see the look on his face and it was not a good one. "Honey, you don't need to be there, I will take April myself there."

"No way, that is a very long drive, we will ask Rose is she could stay with Jimmy again, I will take that day off from work, and we will go together. You have been trying to protect me this whole time, now I will hear it for myself what those monsters did to my little girl. But honey, if you don't mind, I'd like it if we don't talk about it anymore this weekend, lets try to enjoy our time with the children."

"Okay, that's good let's have some fun." The two sat quietly for some drive time. It was like they were in their own thoughts. Then they pulled into the park entrance.

"We are here." Micah shouted loud enough that the children heard him although they had their headphones on watching another movie.

They ripped the headphones off and stared out the window to see what they could see. Looking around to see what was all there for them to do. They began to mentioned what they were seeing.

They found the lot where they had already registered too. Once getting the camper parked. They were able to open the door to it and bring out the large carpet to place on the ground by the entrance.

Once setting everything up, Micah started on the BBQ of hamburgers and Karen had made a potato salad while she was still at home.

April peeled corn on the cob to get that started on the grill, and Jimmy brought out the chairs to sit around the table. Karen started putting the lights on the camper, all the while she was singing songs.

April looked around from where they were parked at. She wanted to make sure that no one was too close to them that were just men.

Karen kept a close eye on her to make sure that she was doing okay, for she knew that she had not gone camping before and she didn't want her to feel afraid of anything.

"I have some burgers that are done now, first come first serve." Micah spoke holding out a plate with a few burgers on it.

Jimmy rushed to his dad, he was hungry and wanted to start on eating. April sat in her chair not moving at all.

"April, come and get you a plate honey. Dad said he has some burgers done, then come and get some potato salad. The corn should be done too." Karen spoke. She watched to see if April was going to get off the chair and get something to eat.

"Mama, are you going to eat?"

"Yes, I am just about done with these lights, give me a couple more minutes." She finished them up and plugged them in. "Lights are on." She said clapping her hands.

April sat in the chair looking at all the pretty lights. "I like them mama, there very pretty.

"Okay what do you say about you and I getting some food. Your dad is just about done with the other burgers in case you want more than one."

April stood up and took the plate her mom was handing to her. She walked over to the table where the food was sitting on. "Okay let's see what I want." She began to put some food on her plate. She then walked back over to the lawn chair that was sitting up against the camper and sat down.

"April, wouldn't you rather sit at the table with the rest of the family?" Karen asked her.

"I guess, I was just making sure that." She stopped what she was saying and walked to the table. She pulled out a chair and sat down. "I was just looking around." she stated.

Karen knew what she was really doing, she wanted to make sure that no one was close to them. She could always tell by the way she was acting that something was wrong with her thinking at the time. "April, you have no need to worry honey, both your dad and I are right here with you and Jimmy." She smiled at her.

There were times where April almost seemed to be a normal child, almost as if nothing bad had ever happened to her. But then the days that were not so nice is what troubled Karen. She hated to see fear written all over her daughter's face. She would do anything to keep that from happening, but as much as she would do for her, she still could see whenever April would be afraid.

They sat around the table eating, laughing and talking. So, after we are done eating, what does everyone want to do?" Micah asked.

"I want to go on the big water slide." Spoke Jimmy.

"What do you want to do April?" Her father asked.

"I'll stay with you and mama."

"I think that you might like the slide too, we will be right there with the both of you the whole time. How about you have some fun and enjoy yourself with your brother?"

"Can I just stay with you and mama?" she asked with fear in her voice.

Karen knew her actions more then Micah did. "Sure, you can honey, you can sit right with your dad and I."

"Okay, that's what I want to do."

Micah never said another word, he knew what his wife said it was for the best. After they cleaned up the table and put things away. They walked to the water slide for Jimmy to have some fun with other kids that were there.

"Go ahead now Jimmy, we will be right here sitting down watching you."

"Okay mama." He ran to the slide and climbed up the tall stairs. He got to the top and looked down at his family sitting close watching him. He slid down it, over and over again. Each time he went down he was laughing and once he reached the bottom, was a swallow pool he went into. He would get out and run around to the side to make that climb again.

April watched him every time he came down, she would smile and laugh almost like she was coming down it too.

Karen watched her daughter smile while she watched Jimmy. "Would you like to try out the slide?"

April looked at her. "Will you stay right here?"

"Of course, I will, I am not leaving anywhere."

April stood up and waited for Jimmy to come down again. Then she followed him to the side and climb it high right behind her brother. Once reaching the top, she looked at her mom and dad sitting there watching her. She gave a little wave to them, then slid down. Landing in the water at the bottom, she let out a laughed that seemed to echo to her mother's ears. She loved the moments that her daughter would find laughter. She knew that she didn't have many of those days now days. She would do anything to erase the bad memories of the past. But for now, she would enjoy watching her laugh and play on the slide with her younger brother.

The children played on the slide for another hour without getting tired. Then it was time for them to go back to their camper for the night. The time had run its course, and it was getting late. Once the darkness set in for the evening, they closed up the slide until the following day.

"Okay kids let's go, it's time to go. They are shutting it down until tomorrow." Karen said.

"Can we come back again tomorrow?" April asked.

"Yes, we can come back again tomorrow. But for now, you both will need a shower before going to bed."

"Awe do we have to go to bed already?" asked Jimmy.

"No, we don't, we can go and start a bon-fire in the pit at the camper and sit around that and sing some songs or we can just talk about things."

"Good because I'm not tired."

They walked back to the camper seeing the lights all lid up. "Micah will you kindly start a fire?" Karen asked.

"Yep, I'm getting right on that. Who wants smores?" he asked. "You did bring things for us to make smore didn't you?"

"I sure did, let me go inside and get them."

The kids waiting outside for their mother to come out. "What's smore?" April asked.

"We made them before honey. It's with gram crackers, roasted marshmallows and Hershey's chocolate."

"I think I remember them." April spoke.

The fire was blazing hot, flames shooting high in the air. "Kids, wait until the fire goes down some before roasting your marshmallows." Micah warned them.

The children put their marshmallows on their stick and sat around the camp fire waiting for it to go down some. It was hot enough that everyone slid their chairs future away. After waiting for several minutes, the fire went down enough to put the sticks in the fire to burn their marshmallows.

"Here is your chocolate and gram cracker. Hurry while its hot so it will melt your chocolate." Karen said.

The kids hurried and put their hot marshmallow on their gram crackers. They started to eat their smores, while they were pipping hot. "Humm that is good, can I have another one?" Jimmy asked.

"No son that is enough for the night. To many sweets you won't be sleeping."

"We will sit around the fire for a little while longer, then we will call it a night. It's getting late, and if we were home, we all would already be in bed."

"Okay dad." Jimmy said.

After the fire died down more, it was time for showers then bed. "Jimmy, you get in the shower first, then April can get in it."

"Okay mama." He went into the camper to get his pajamas and shower. He was getting tired, knowing that his dad was right when he said he would be in bed if he was at home.

"April did you like your smores?"

"Yes, I did. I think there good but sweet."

Karen chucked, "yes sweet they are and your brother wanted another one."

"I can't even eat two of them, and he wants to eat two."

"You need to get your clothes for tonight, and remember what we talked about where you're going to be sleeping at."

"Yes mama, you won't be going anywhere, will you?"

"No honey I am staying right here, your father and I are headed to bed too. After you get your shower, and all tucked into bed, we are also going to bed."

"Okay, I think Jimmy is out now, I will go and get mine." She walked away and went into the camper.

"Do you think that she will be alright?" Micah asked.

"Do you mean for the night, or in general?"

"Both I guess."

"I'm going to keep her going to see Ellie, and I think once she goes to court and see's that those men are going to prison for a very long time, I think that is going to help her that much more."

"I hope so, I just want her all better and for her to feel safe again without all the worrying."

"I do too. Why don't we go inside now. While she is in the shower, we can get in our night clothes."

"Okay I'm coming, I just want to make sure that the fire is out completely."

"Okay I will see you in a few minutes."

Micah started to put the rest of the fire out, so he could join his wife. It felt like a life time since he laid next to her. He missed cuddling her in his arms.

10

Their weekend was over and they were headed back home. The children had the best of times swimming playing putt putt golf, and sliding down the water slide. Karen and Micah had the best of time with both of their children together. Micah had promised the children once school was out, they would come for a whole week camping.

"Do you think that April will go back to her own bed now, I mean she did sleep in the bunkbed although I know Jimmy was on top bunk."

"She might be able too, but remember she did wake up making some noise, although it was nothing like she was doing at home. Honey let me talk with her about it, I want her to be able to sleep in her own room now too."

What neither of them knew, is although April had headphones on her head, she did not have the movie playing in her ear, she was listening to everything that her parents were saying. It made her feel sad, knowing that her father was not having the best of sleep ever since he was staying in her bedroom at night. She felt sorry that she had taken his side of the bed, and sleeping in her parent's room ever since she had come home. She knew that although she still felt fear, she needed to go back to her own room and allow her father to come back to his.

After reaching home, the children carried in their clothes, and Karen did the cold food that belonged in the refrigerator. She was tired and just wanted sleep, but she knew that she needed to talk to April about going to sleep in her own room.

"April, can I speak with you for a minute honey."

"Okay, April walked over to her mother knowing what she was going to ask of her, so she quickly spoke up before giving her mother a chance to ask. "Mama, can I go sleep in my own room tonight, I think that I'm ready too?"

This shocked Karen, she did not expect to hear that at all. She put her hand over her mouth, and a few tears fell down her cheeks. "Wow, April,

I am so surprised. Yes, honey you can go sleep in your own room, this will be a very good thing to try and do honey. I believe that you are ready, you slept quite well in the bunkbed, all on your own."

April knew she slept on her own, although Jimmy was just above her. But she knew that she was putting stress on both of her parents, which she never wanted to do to them. She had a loving mother and father and was blessed to have the both of them. "Yeah mama, I did sleep by myself." She smiled at her mother, but inside she had a fear hit her, what if she woke up screaming again, what then shall she do?

"Okay honey very good, I will let your father know that its okay for him to come back into our bedroom tonight." she smiled at April then gave her a little kiss on her cheek. "You may want to get some sleep honey, it's really getting late, I will be up in a minute and say your prayers with you."

"Okay mama." She turned and walked away slowly. A tear dripped down her cheek. She felt somewhat a relief, but in another way, she felt fear. She had slept with her mother ever since she had some home, and she had been home for nearly a month now. *"God please don't let me be afraid to sleep by myself, don't let me wake up screaming." She prayed silently.*

Walking into her room, she changed her clothing and put on her pajamas. Pulling back the covers to her bed, she felt a slight fear grip her heart. She was now alone, like she was when she was there at the place she was raped and beaten. She knew that she had heard her parents speak from their heart about what they wanted, and she knew that it was time for her to give her father back his own space to be with her mother. But the thoughts of being alone, really bothered her. But how can she take back what she had already told her mother, how can she say that she still felt like she needed to sleep in the bed with her mother? She climbed in her bed, eyes wide open so big, her heart began to race fast. She sat up quickly, placing her hand over her heart. She needed to get a grip, and not allow what happened to her, keep playing a big part of her. She just wished that she could sleep with her mother forever, so she never had to feel that fear again. The fear that Kevin or one of his evil men were going to come in her room again and rape her over and over again. A fear where she is in a room that was made for her to be attacked by men and made to do such wicked evil things with them, so much that when they raped her behind, she couldn't sit down for days, and she bleed from her butt. The thought came rushing back to her, and brough fear back.

She felt like as long as she was able to sleep in her mother's room with her, she didn't have to think about that happening all over again. Now it was up to her, to get past all of those thoughts, and she knew that her parents never understood all that she had gone through, because she had only told them parts of what has happened to her.

She laid back down and closed her eyes tight, hoping by squeezing then shut, she wouldn't see the men that hurt her.

Karen walked in her room. Not knowing the turmoil that April was fighting at the time, she walked over to her bed, and leaning over her and kissed her forehead. "Dear Jesus, I ask that you help April sleep very good tonight, take away all fear and anxiety. Remove everything that comes to torment her mind in Jesus name amen. Good night my sweet little girl."

"Good night mama, I love you."

"I love you too, now I need to go and say Jimmy's prayers with him. Would you like the nightlight left on?"

"Yes please." She watched as her mother slipped through the other side of the door. She felt instant fear grip her heart and thoughts. Then she remembered the prayer her mother just spoke over her. *"Stop this right now April, mama just prayed over you and you are strong, you are safe, and you are no longer at Kevins. You are happy, and you are free."* She reminded herself, talking out loud. That was one of the things that Mrs. Walker had taught her, she told her to speak out loud to the fear, and it had to go and leave her. She told her that whenever she felt scared like she was still at Kevins and the men were there to abuse her again, to speak out loud and remind herself that she was safe at home with her parents. So, she started to do that, she never felt like she needed to when she was sleeping next to her mother, but now that she is back in her own bedroom, she felt that it was that time to start reminding herself where she was at.

Karen laid in bed, wondering how April was doing all alone in her own bed. She hoped and prayed that she would be able to sleep all night long without waking up screaming or being afraid.

Karen and Micah were happy to be able to be together again, their whole married life, they had not spent a night without each other, until April came home and that all changed. It felt so good to have her husband's arms wrapped around her again. It was a feeling that she never wanted to go without again. Her and Micah talked for a while, before falling to sleep.

Morning came and Karen went to go walk up Jimmy for school, but when she opened his door to his bedroom, she did not expect to see what she did. April was sleeping in his bed with him. It touched heart to think that she came into her brother's room during the night, rather then wake her up screaming again. "Jimmy" she spoke softly hoping not to disturb April. "It's time to get up for school."

"Can't I stay home today, I'm so tired."

"No, you only have two days left of school, then you are out for the summer."

Jimmy peeled himself out from the covers, he looked at his sister sleeping in his bed. "She came in here last night, she said she didn't want to wake you up. She asked me if she could sleep in here, I told her it was okay." He looked at his mom.

"Thank you, Jimmy for letting her come in here. She has gone through a hard time when she was gone away from us."

"I know mama." Although they never spoke about things in front of him, he knew by watching some of her actions, that she was hurting.

"Get dressed and let her sleep, after your done, come down stairs to eat."

"Okay."

Karen went down stair to start making breakfast for her son and husband. Micah had the coffee already going. "Honey you would not believe what I just seen."

"What was that?"

She told him what she seen when she went in their son's room.

"Oh no, are you kidding me, I didn't hear a thing during the night, did you?"

"No, I don't think she woke up screaming or anything like that, I think she must have just woken up, and went into his room because she felt afraid."

"What do you think that we should do?"

"We go to court in three days, lets see what happens between now and then. Maybe we should just allow her to go into Jimmys room and sleep if she feels the need too."

"But how does Jimmy like that? I mean what if it gets him upset with her, we don't want that either."

"I don't think that it will, he may be only six years old, but he's far from stupid. He knows that something is not right, he has seen some of the things that she had done before, although she is getting much better."

Jimmy walked into the kitchen. He looked at his mom and dad. "April came in my room last night; I think she was afraid to be alone."

"Did that make you feel sad that she came in there?"

"What do you mean dad?"

"Did it bother you that she came in your room?"

"No, I knew she needed me."

Micah looked at Karen and gave a smile. "I'm glad that it never bothered you son, she has gone through a lot of things that had hurt her very bad. She does need all of us to help her."

"It's okay if she sleeps in my room, I don't mind."

"Thank you for helping your sister out like that." Micah rubbed the top of Jimmys head.

"Okay you better eat up, your dad is going to take you to school and I will pick you up. Remember in a couple of days you will be able to sleep in school will be out for the summer."

"Good, April is lucky she doesn't have to go to school."

Karen looked at Micah and gave a slight grin, she knew that Jimmy just did not understand what was really going on and why his sister had not gone back to school yet.

She was hoping that by the end of the summer, that April would be ready to go back to school and feel like her old self again, that everything she had gone through would be far behind her.

After her husband and son left for the day, she wanted to spend some time in prayer before April came down stairs.

Kneeling next to the couch, she began to let out her hearts cry to the Lord. She was an emotional wreck about what was going to take place during the court hearing. She never wanted April to know how she really felt about her little girl having to stand up in court and face the men that abused her so badly. She was just a nine-year-old little girl, and the thoughts of her having to testify was mortifying to her. She wished that her daughter never had to go through that kind of humiliation, seeing the men that raped her and beat her was just a terrible feeling. She knew that April had agreed to go to court and face those men, and tell of what they had done to her, but she also knew that it was going to be unsettling in her to do such a thing. *"Oh God, I hate that my little girl has to face those evil men. I hate what they have done to her, and I know Jesus, you hate it too. God help my baby girl to be strong and not afraid.*

Help her to over come everything that happened to her. Lord place your gentle touch on my girl, let her feel your arms wrap all around her during the night, where she feels safe enough to sleep in her own room, where she is happy and full of life in Jesus, name amen." When she opened her eye's April was standing there. "April, honey how long have you been standing there?"

"I heard you talking to God mama." She walked over to her mother and sat down on her lap, while her mother was still on the floor. "I'm sorry mama, I didn't want that bad man to take me away from you."

"Oh no honey, you have nothing to be sorry about, you did nothing wrong at all. It was those bad men that did the wrong. April, I never want you to ever think that you were bad, honey please, I prayed that Jesus will help you to be so happy again, like you used to be. It hurts me so much knowing that men hurt you and did so many bad things to you."

"But I make you cry mama."

Karen held her close and she started to weep. "Its not you that makes me cry honey, its what happened to you that makes mama cry. I wish I could take all the pain away from you, but I can't, that's why I pray and ask Jesus to take it away from you. I want you to be so happy, and enjoy your life, I hate to see when you're not happy and you feel scared and even afraid to sleep in your own bed. But I want you to know, I don't blame you for anything at all, and neither does your father."

April laid her head on her mother's shoulders. "I love you mama, and I'm happy that you and daddy came to get me and bring me back home."

"I'm so happy to have you back with us again, and your father is too honey, he can sleep so much better knowing that you are safe with us now."

"But what about when I took his side of the bed, and he took my bed. I think I made him mad at me."

"April you must not think like that, your father has not ever been mad at you for that. He just has a hard time sleeping in your bed, when he has been used to his own bed. But he never once blamed you for that, he understood why you felt scared. He knew that you slept with your brother last night and he wondered if maybe you should come back in with me."

"He did?" she asked and her eyes got very big. "What did you say?"

"I told him that you would rather him sleep in his own bed, and that you can still sleep in Jimmys bed for as long as you and he don't mind." She wanted to let her know that she wanted her husband to have his own bed, but yet she could still sleep in her brother's bed if she needed too.

"It's okay mama, I will stay with Jimmy if he doesn't mind." She smiled. I know that daddy needs his big bed, and not my little one."

"Thank you, my sweet girl." She hugged her tight. "You are very special to me; I love you so much."

"I love you to mama. When I go and see Mrs. Walker next time, I'm going to tell her that I am not sleeping in your bed anymore."

"Good for you." She could tell that she was proud to have given the bed back to her daddy.

11

The day arrived for April to face the evil men in court. She seemed to know what she was going to say, but she really had no idea of what kind of questions the prosecutor was going to be asking, nor did her mother and father know what all was about to come out. None of them could have known just what would be said during the hearing.

Arriving to the court house, they noticed right away, that the news media was standing outside of the court room. There were several television news stations standing around. Micah did not want her daughter to walk by any of them, and have her face plastered all over the news. He asked Karen to find something that would cover her whole face and head. He knew all to well what the news media does to people, all in the name of it's their job someone has to do it. To a point he could understand that, but when it came time to the heinous crime of what had been committed with his daughter, he knew that he needed to protect her as much as possible. Karen looked around in the car to see what she could find, when all she could find was a large scarf.

"April, I will need to cover your face and head with this honey. There are a lot of people out there that will want to see who you are knowing that today is the day those men will be prosecuted. I don't want them to harass you at all. So come here before we get out of the car, I need to cover you up."

April listened to her mother, her heart seemed to race at the thoughts that soon she would be seeing the same men that had did so much wrong to her, and causing her to go through painful memories of what they had done to her. She leaned forward to have her mother cover her.

Karen started to wrap her daughter's face and head into the scarf, trying to leave her plenty of room to breathe. "There I think that she's covered good enough so no one will be able to see who she is, don't you honey?" she asked her husband.

Micah looked over her well. "Yes, I don't see how they will be able to see her face at all. April are you able to breathe good under that?"

"Yes daddy, I can breathe."

"Good we better get in there now, I'm not sure where we are to go, once we are on the inside, and we don't want to be late. We have to go and speak to Mr. Tibbs before going into the court room."

"Who is he?" Karen asked.

"That's the prosecutor's name."

"Oh, okay well we better get going then." She opened her door, then the back door for April. "Just hold onto my hand the who time, I will lead you into where we have to go."

"Okay mama, hold my hand tight okay."

"I will baby."

The three started to walk across the street, when Micah noticed the policemen were bringing in several men with cuffs on their hands and chains on their ankles. He wondered if they could have been the men that hurt his daughter. They were Mexican by the looks of them, and he knew that April had mentioned to him and his wife about brown men that spoke in another language held her against her will. Just looking at those men, caused him to feel so much anger on the inside of him. Without paying attention to what he was saying, he spoke out loud. "Jesus help me"

Karen looked at him to see what was wrong. He motioned to her the men. Karen looked to where he pointed, and when she seen them, she felt sick to her stomach, then a rage came all over on the inside of her. She felt like she was about to vomit. She held onto her stomach. "Jesus help us." She then spoke, turning her head away from looking at the men. She knew that she needed to be strong for April, and she had to think of her best interest and not one of her own.

"What's the matter?" April asked.

"We are praying honey; we need his help today with all of this." She didn't want to lie to her daughter, but she knew she couldn't tell her about seeing those men either. So, she spoke the truth, but withheld all of what she was praying for.

"Okay April we have to walk up many steps, so you hold your mother's hand, okay?"

"Okay daddy." She gripped her mother's hand tighter.

When the people of the media seen them starting to walk up the steps, several came rushing down to them putting the microphone up to their mouths. "Can you tell me if this is one of the children that was taken and put into child sex slavery?"

That statement angered both Micah and Karen. They didn't say a word, but tried to push them away from April.

"Can you tell us what happened to your child?" another one asked.

"Please we deserve the right to know what happened to your child. Can you tell us anything?" A woman yelled placing the microphone to Micah's mouth.

"Sure, I can tell you something. I want all of you to leave me and my family alone. We have gone through way too much to have all of you vultures coming after us. Now leave us alone." He shouted. Pushing back the people with his arms, and allowing Karen and April to walk up some steps, someone reached down and grabbed the scarf off from April's head, revealing her face. Karen hurried and hid her face in her clothing. With a mother's protection over her child, she faced the man that tore it off from April. "I can only hope and pray that you never will have to go through what my daughter and my family has been going through for two years. Now this is the last time, back off and leave us alone." She spoke with anger but yet authority.

The men and women heard her loud and clear, they did back off, she watched as they stepped aside and allowed them to finish climbing the steps. She could hear some complain, but then she heard a man's voice saying "just let them be. Give them their space."

She was happy that they decided to leave them alone, she knew that April had already gone through so much hell on earth, that she hated the thoughts of the media doing anything to jeopardize just how far she has come, she didn't want any set-backs.

Once reaching the top of the steps, Micah opened the door. There was a man standing there waiting for them. "Hello, are you the Davis's?"

"Yes, we are."

"I thought for a minute I was going to have to come down there and help you out, but whatever your wife said to the people, stopped them in their tracks. The media is terrible when it comes time for people needing their privacy."

"Yes, I gathered that." Micah gave a slight grin. "We are here to meet Mr. Tibbs."

"That would be me." He held out his hand to shake Micah's. "Follow me, we have enough time to go over a few things before we head into the court room." He looked down at April.

"You must be the brave little girl I've been hearing all about."

April looked up at him and smiled. "I'm April."

"I know that you are honey, I am so happy that you decided to come here today. We will do our very best to get every one of those men that hurt you locked away forever."

"I hope so."

He opened the door to a room that only had chairs a table and pen and paper. "Have a seat everyone, I'd like to go over just a couple of things before we head into the court room. Today April, you will be called to take the stand." He looked at her how she clung tightly to her mother. "I know that this might seem a little scary, but after today, there should be no longer need to have to come back to court. If we play our cards well today, the men will be put away for a very long time. Once your name is called, you will be asked to take the stand. Once you are sitting down, they will ask you to tell the truth and only the truth. Then you will respond saying yes. Then a lawyer for those men, will be asking you questions."

"You mean to tell me that those men will have a lawyer to depend them, of what they did to my daughter?"

"As much as you and I may hate the law when it comes time for allowing men like that the right to an attorney, that is the law. We have to for the people that have committed the most heinous crime a chance to fight their case. I hate it and I know that you do too."

"Is there a chance that they could get off?" Micah asked.

Mr. Tibbs looked at April, then back to Micah. "I wish that I could say there is no chance for that to happen. But I cannot say that, what I can say, is that I do not believe for one minute that the jury will not find each person guilty of rape and selling children for sex. That is why we need your daughter to paint an ugly picture of every person involved today. The worst picture that is painted, the more the jury will see the need to send them all away for many, many years. People like that need to never see the light again, that way the children will be protected from these kinds of people." He looked at April. "I know that this may seen very scary for you to do, but honey, if you can be strong to sit on the chair and face the people in the court room, and tell us all what they did to you and anyone else that you saw, we can get them locked up for a very long time. Do you think that you can do that?" April first looked at her mother, before answering him.

"We will be right there honey that whole time." Karen spoke knowing that her little girl was scared.

"Yes, I can do it."

"Okay good, we need to head on over to the courtroom now. You can sit anywhere that you like, and when your name is called, you will walk up to the front and sit down in the chair okay?"

"Okay." She squeezed her mother's hand.

Karen looked down at her daughter, its alright honey, I know that you can do this."

"Okay let's get in there now."

They followed Mr. Tibbs to the court room, once the door was opened up, April could see several people she knew from when she was held at Kevins. She felt so frightened, that she pulled herself back.

Karen felt how she jerked her arm back. "April." She spoke in a soft voice getting down low to be April's size. "Remember honey, why we are here. We need to have all of these men put away. We do not want them to walk away to be able to hurt anyone else ever again, do we?"

"No mama."

"Okay, are you sure that you're going to be able to do this?"

April looked in the court room again and seen the wicked men that had hurt her. Tears fell down her cheeks, her mother watched her wipe them away. "Yes, mama I can do it."

Micah hated to see grown men sitting in the same room as he was, knowing that they raped his little girl. A sweet little child his child being manhandled so wickedly. They found seats to sit down on.

April tried not to look towards the men, then when the judge walked in, everyone stood up until the judge sat down. The judge stated speaking about the case, when April heard her name called, she looked to the front of the room. She wasn't being called up to speak yet, it was just the judge mentioning her name, so everyone knew who would be speaking against the men.

After Mr. Tibbs stood up, and he spoke about why they were all in the court room today. Then he looked back at April. "I'd like to call April Davis to the stand." He watched as April stood up and started to walk to the front. She stood in front of the chair, "raise your right hand, do you swear to tell the truth and nothing but the truth so help you God?"

"Yes."

"You may be seated." The judge told her.

April looked at the judge, then sat down.

Mr. Tibbs stood in front of April trying to keep her from having to stare at the men, he knew that she was very frightened. "April I'm going to ask you some questions, now I want you to take your time when answering them. We must know everything that you can remember what happened to you, okay?"

"Okay."

"Can you tell me how you come to know Kevin Gutierrez?"

April looked to where Kevin was sitting at, she then looked at Mr. Tibbs. "I was walking home from school, when a man kidnapped me and took me to Kevin's."

"When this man that kidnapped you, were you scared?"

"Yes." She answered and started to cry softly.

"April, I know that this is hard for you to answer me, but we must know the facts about what all took place. Can we keep going?"

"Yes." She spoke looking back to her mom and dad.

"Okay, that man that picked you up, is he here today?"

She looked at all the men that were sitting in orange with cuffs on their hands, and chains on their ankles. "No."

"You have stated that the man took you to Kevin's, is Kevin here today?"

She looked once again at the men. "Yes."

"Can you point him out to us?"

"Right there." She pointed to Kevin.

Mr. Tibbs looked at Kevin. "That is the man that held you against your will for two years, far away from your mother and father?"

"Yes." She started to cry again; this time Mr. Tibbs gave her a hanky.

"I'm sorry this hurts you so much, but we need the people to know what Kevin did to you. Can you tell us what Kevin did?"

"He beat me." She sniffled.

"Can you tell me how many times that he beat you?"

"I don't know, because sometimes he had Travis beat me too."

"So, it wasn't just Kevin that beat you, he also had other people beat you?"

The lawyer for Kevin stood up. "He's leading the witness, she already said Travis, not others."

"Okay, April how many others beat you while you were at Kevin's, can you tell us that?" he reworded it for her.

"I'm not sure, but I know I was beat-up a lot of times by men. Travis beat me a lot."

"Can you tell us why Kevin had Travis beat you?"

"Because" she sniffled. "I didn't want to have sex with men."

"He had Travis beat you up, because you didn't want to have sex with men." He looked towards the juries. "I cannot imagine what it was like for a seven-year-old little girl to be taken away from a loving family, placed into the hands of men that would beat her all because she did not want to have sex with them. "Can you tell us, how they beat you?"

"Travis beat me so bad one time that I almost died. He punched me in my face and head, he kicked me all over my body. He threw me into the wall and onto the floor. He broke my arm."

At this time Micah was sitting towards the back, and felt himself getting very angry. Karen took a hold of his hand and gave it a tight squeeze. She had tears coming down her face.

"He did all of that to you because Kevin asked him too?"

"Kevin got mad at him, because I almost died and he couldn't let any men come in and see me until I was healed."

He continued to ask her more questions, all the while Micah was having a hard time listening to what his daughter had gone through.

"April now we need to know, when Kevin had men come into your room to be with you, what did those men do to you?"

"They hurt me."

"We need to know how the men hurt you."

"They made me have sex with them. Some of them got mad at me because I didn't want to touch them."

"Where did these men want you to touch them? Can you tell us about that?"

"Some of them wanted me to undress them, and then undress myself in front of them. Some of them wanted me to touch there you know what." She couldn't bring herself to saying it.

"When you talk about touching their you know what, can you tell me if you are referring to their private parts?"

"Yes."

"What else did they want you to do for them that you didn't want too?"

"Some wanted me to bend over so they can hurt me in my butt."

When Karen and Micah heard that, it sickened them so badly.

They could not believe their daughter went through so much pain from grown men. Karen squeezed his hands so tight, that it nearly drew blood, without her paying attention, her nails went into his skin.

He sat there crying over what he was hearing that his little girl went through.

"April, I need you to tell the court what else these men did to you."

"Some times Kevin sent in two men at one time to come and rape me." She started to weep very hard at mentioning what happened to her.

Micah stood up and yelled, he was so angry. "How can anyone do this to a child, you rotten men all need to die." He yelled out.

The judge asked that a bailer take Mr. Davis out of the court room. He could see that it was to much for the father to listen too.

Karen sat there, although she too wanted to scream, she knew that she needed to sit there for her daughter. She promised her that she would be right there for her.

Mr. Tibbs seen that Mr. Davis was taken out of the room, so he continued to ask questions.

"Can you tell me if you recognize any of these other men sitting over here?"

"Yes."

"Can you tell us who they are and what they did?"

"That's Travis, he beat me the most, and forced me to have sex with him and other man."

"So, Travis not only beat you up, but he also forced you into having sex with him and also another man?"

"Your honor, she had already stated that is what took place.

"So noted." The judge said.

"Can you tell me about any of the other ones?"

April started to name each person by name, and what part they played.

"Can you tell me what Tina did?"

"She would bring me in some food to eat, most of it was nasty, and I didn't know what she fed me."

"Is that all that she did?"

"No, she told me that she was going to be having men come in to see me, and if I didn't do what they wanted, then I would not be able to eat. I'd also be beaten by the men or Travis."

"Did you ever go without food?"

"Yes, a lot of times."

"Now when you say that you went without food, how long of a time did you go without eating?"

"Sometimes three days."

Karen sat listening to the horror of what her daughter told the court. She never knew a lot of what she was hearing, and it was tearing her up on the inside.

"April when these men would come in to have sex with you, how often did that happen, was it like once a day, two or three times a day?"

"No, it was fifty or sixty times a day men would come to rape me."

That took Mr. Tibbs by surprise. "Wow, are you telling us that men would come into your room fifty-sixty times a day and rape you?"

"Yes."

"Were there more children there then just yourself?"

"Yes, there were a lot of children there."

"Can you tell us anything about the other children?"

"Yes, at first I thought that only girls were there, then one day I looked out my room, and see three boy's hands tied up to rope, they were being pulled down the hallway to the end. That's where the boys were kept at."

"Did you ever talk with any of them? Or did you ever see any of them with men?"

"Yes, I did see them with the men, I heard them screaming so loud, that I started to scream and cry."

"Why did you scream and cry?"

"Because I knew what was happening to them. I knew that men were raping them. One day after the screams, I seen a boy walk by my door, bleeding bad from his butt." She started to cry at the thoughts of what happened to the boy.

"Can you tell the court if there was another time that you see a boy?"

"Yes, I looked out my door, when I heard some people talking low, I wanted to see why. When I looked, I seen two men carrying out a little boy by his hands and feet."

"Two men carried out a boy, do you know why he was being carried out?"

"He was dead."

Mr. Tibbs asked her more questions. And she did her best to remember what happened.

"Was there a time that you spoke with a little girl across the hallway from you?"

April thought about the little girl she was suppose to talk too, but she didn't know how Mr. Tibbs heard about that. "Yes, there was a girl that Kevin told me that I needed to tell her what her job would be. He told me to tell her if she didn't have sex with the men, then she would not be able to eat, and she would be beaten."

"Did you tell her what Kevin asked you to tell her?"

"Yes."

"Then what happened?"

"She was scared, and didn't want to have sex with them. She wanted to go home to her mom."

"What happened after that?"

"Kevin had Travis beat me again."

"What for?"

"Because I told her that it hurts and I hated it there, and I wanted to go home too."

"Did you ever see that girl again?"

"Yes."

"When?"

"She died, and I seen two men carry her out."

After April was asked many questions about what she had gone through and what she witnessed other children go through, she was asked to go and sit down next to her mother. Her mother wrapped her arms around her so tight. "I'm so sorry baby, you never told me a lot of what happened to you."

"I wanted to forget it."

After the jury came back, they had given Kevin and his men life without the possibility of parole.

12

Once leaving the building, they had long since forgotten about the mob of people waiting to hear something on the outside. They opened the door with April walking like a normal child, when several people came rushing to her side, with several mikes placed into her face. Karen looked at Micah, Micah felt like he needed to say something to the people.

He put his hand up like to tell them to quiet down. "I will say something here."

"Can you tell us what did the men get for time?"

"I can say they all deserve death, but they did not get that. Those men are evil animals; they don't deserve to live for what they have done to my daughter and other children. I was removed from the court room because I hated what they did to my girl."

"They removed you, why did that happen?" someone asked.

"Because I got angry and started to shout at them. I'm her father, I couldn't just sit there hearing what kind of things they did to her. They are evil men and none of them deserve to live. How can someone take a child, and sell them to men over and over again just for money. What ever happened to getting a job, and making an honest living. I think we need to bring back the death penalty by hanging."

Karen could hear the heartbreak her husband was talking. It hurt her to hear the words that he was using. She had never known him to be so angry before and it scared her to think if something doesn't change soon on the inside of him, she would lose the man she married. She tried to get him to walk away from the crowd of people. But they were all waiting for more, like hungry wolves. Feeding on a man's bitterness and pain.

"What kind of time did they get?"

"They each got life without a chance of parole." Karen spoke. "Now please allow us our time and move out of the way."

"We need to bring hanging back; I would personally hang each one of them." Micah yelled out like a mad man.

Karen could tell by his actions that he needed help, maybe by Ellie. She could see ever since he was in the courtroom and heard some of the things that April said that it was ripping Micah's heart out. That was why she never told him in the first place about the things that she did know. "Let us go, Micah enough said, lets go." She spoke in a way to him she had never done before. He looked at her and knew that she meant business. He pushed past the mob and they walked down the long steps.

A man came from behind them and handed them a card. "This is my contact, if you ever want to give your story, give me a call. I will have you come on television and I'll give you an interview about what happened."

Micah looked at the man and took his card, then he reached in his pocket. "Here, this is my business card, in case I forget to call you, you can reach out to me. I have plenty to say."

"Okay, thank you, I'll do just that."

On the way home everyone was in their own little world, no one saying anything. They drove for miles in their own thoughts, not speaking a word.

"Mama" April broke the silence.

"Yes darling." She turned around to look at her.

"Are you and daddy mad at me?"

"Mad at you, why would we be mad at you?"

"Because of what I said in court."

"Honey we can never be mad at you because of what happened to you. Your father and I don't blame you for that. We know you never wanted any of that to happen to you. Honey, we know that the men that did that stuff to you, are the bad ones."

"You don't blame me then?"

"No honey we don't blame you. We hate what happened to you, we are happy that they are going to prison for a long, long time."

"How long will they go to prison for mama?"

"The judge said that they are going to do life in prison without a chance for parole."

"Does that mean they will be there forever?"

"I think that means they will be in prison for twenty-five years. I think that's what they call life."

"I'm glad they get to go for a longtime mama, are you happy too?"

"I'm very happy they will be locked up for a long time."

April sat there quiet for a few minutes, then she leaned up and started to talk again. "Daddy."

"Yes honey, what's on your mind?"

"Are you mad at me?"

"No April I am not mad at you at all. Why would you think that I was mad at you?"

"You got mad in the court room daddy. You started to yell and they made you leave the room."

Karen looked at her husband, wondering what he was going to say. "April when I heard some of the things that those men did to you, it broke my heart. I wanted to strangle them for what they did to you."

"Then you don't blame me daddy?"

"No honey I sure don't blame you at all. You are my daughter, my little girl, and I don't blame you."

"I remember some more things since we left there."

Karen looked at her daughter wondering what else could there be? She had already told so much of the filthy things she and others had went through, what else possibly could be told.

"I for got to tell them, how they beat a girl to death."

Karen put her hand over her mouth, she didn't want to scream at the thoughts of them grown men killing a child by beating her. "Why would they do that to a child honey?"

"Her name was Bryanna; she was six years old. She started to scream and kick around when they tried having sex with her, so they kept hitting her until she just died."

Karen had tears coming down her cheeks, Micah was mortified. It was hard to imagine people could be so wicked to such little children that all they wanted was love and being taken care of.

"How did you know this happened to her honey?" Karen asked between sobs.

"They made me watch them do that." She had tears fall down her cheeks at remembering the hurt and pain of what the little girl went through.

"Why in the world would they want you to watch that? Wasn't it enough what they were already doing to you?" Karen cried out in not wanting to hear anymore evil of what these men had done. She hated to hear and know what happened to her daughter, but in another sense, she knew that she had to allow April to talk about it, and not keep it bottled up on the inside.

"They told me, that if I didn't start doing my job better and stop fighting the men that came into my room, then that is what was going to happen to me." She let out a couple loud cries.

When Micah heard her start crying hard, he pulled the car over and asked Karen to get in the back with her and comfort her. He hated to know what had happened to his daughter, but yet he never heard all of it because he was forced to leave the courtroom. He felt it just as well that he didn't know all of it, because what he did know was enough that he had wished death on the men that did that when he was at the courtroom. He hated the thoughts that was going through his mind, they were not thoughts of anything good but evil. He knew that he needed to get a grip on how he was feeling, otherwise, he would become so out raged with things in life that he would become no good to his family. He could hear the voice of God trying to cut through the darkness he had allowed to come in. His soul was vexed with hate and evil thoughts towards those men that hurt his daughter. He turned some calm music on and turning it up just a little so he could talk to God without his family in the back seat hearing what he was about to say. *"God, I need your help right now, my thoughts have gone to evil. I hate those man that I that did that, and I don't want to feel hate like this. Father, I know that you see what I am thinking and feeling, please help me to gather my thoughts to not be hating man such as I do right now. Help me to hate their sin, but not the man. God, please help me I beg you; I hate myself, and I don't want to carry this hate around with me. I want to see good once again, but right now I only see what they did to my daughter."* He poured his heart and soul out to God knowing that at this time, he was filled with darkness he never thought was possible. As he drove and talked with God, he went into a beautiful vision and he heard the voice of God speaking to him. He seen a beautiful garden full of the most beautiful flowers he had ever seen before. There were beautiful butterflies that were flying around, and landing on flowers. He drove looking at the garden that was right in front of him. It was like he could stretch his hand out and touch them, they were so close. The beauty of what he was looking at with beautiful stones placed all around for one to walk on throughout the garden. Then he heard the voice of God clearly. *"I will give this garden to your daughter as a healing to many others. She will be forever changed, once she has learned to forgive everyone that has hurt her. I will raise her up to help the broken hearted, even at a tender age that she is. I am doing a work on the inside of her, and I will make the fine correction of the heart. This garden you will also have a part in my son, I say learn to forgive those that you feel doesn't deserve life. I will show you the plans I have for you and your family."* He came out of the vision. At that very moment, he broke in tears, but they were not tears of what those men had done to his daughter this time, they were tears of what God showed him and spoke to him. He turned off the music to talk with his family. "Honey, I need you and April to forgive me for my actions. I'm so sorry I lost my head there, both in the courtroom and out of it, when I was talking to the people outside. Please forgive me."

Karen was happy that he now seemed calmed and asking for forgiveness, maybe he wouldn't have to seek help. Maybe he just had to have a little time to think about his actions. "I forgive you honey."

"I do too daddy."

Micah got all choke up hearing his little girl say that she forgives him too. He knew that because he acted out in court that's what caused him to be thrown out of the room, to where he could not be there for her. "Thank both of you for forgiving me for the terrible things that I said. I know now that I was just allowing the devil to use me to talk so wickedly. No matter what anyone does, it's not my place to wish death, but it is my place to asked God to get ahold of their heart. I just feel terrible for how I behaved."

"Honey we all have done things that we are ashamed for doing them, if you have repented to God, then you know that he is good to forgive you."

"I turned the music on for a reason." He stopped what he was saying. "Before I go on with that, is anyone hungry?"

"Yes, honey we are very hungry."

"It's been hours since we had a bite to eat. We left the house at five in the morning, and look at the time now. It's nearly three now. We should go get something to eat?"

"At this point it doesn't matter, we are just hungry."

Micah looked at the town they were driving through. "I see a restaurant just up ahead, should we go there?"

Karen looked out to where ahead was. "Yes, it looks nice."

Micah pulled in the parking lot. "When we place our order's, I want to tell you what happened when I turned the music on in the car."

"Okay." Karen gave him a smile. She knew that something had changed him from being in a deep rage, to being calm. This she had to hear, knowing that something had to of happened.

They took their seats that the waitress took them too, after looking over the menu's, they placed their orders. Karen looked right at Micah waiting to hear what happened to him that changed the way he was acting.

Micah noticed that she was looking at him in a strange way. "Okay, I know you want to hear what happened." He looked at April knowing she was really too young to understand, although she had gone through so much over the last two years that most adults will never go through. "I know you knew that I had reached a point of desperation. I don't know if you can quite understand just what was going on inside of me. I became so outraged with what happened." He looked at April without saying her name.

"I know you did honey." Karen said looking at him, she did understand it, she too felt like that at some point.

"You see as her father; it was my job to protect her. And when I couldn't do that, I felt so much like a failure. I couldn't let you down as a husband and a father to Jimmy, but inside I was being so tore up over our little girl not being home with us. There were times at work I just sat there behind my desk and not even answer the phone when it rang. But some of the guys I have working for me, knew that I was hurting, and they helped me out. They would answer and take the orders that people called in to make. They only reason I even still got up in the morning and forced myself to go to work were because of you, Jimmy and the hope that our April would be coming home to us."

"You never told me any of that."

"I couldn't, I had to be strong for my family, and while I was at work falling apart, my men helped me do the work that I no longer could."

"What happened in the car." She wanted to know what changed him.

"I was very angry, I needed help again, to keep me from losing it altogether. I turned the music on, I looked in the back and seen how you were hugging April. She needed you at the time, while I needed God. I cried out to God in a way I never have before. I felt so much hate." He looked around him to make sure that no one was within ear shot of hearing him. They clearly would not understand what he was talking about. I told God I needed his help, because I scared myself so bad. All of a sudden God took me into a vision while I was driving." His eyes teared up just the thoughts of how wonderful God was to him.

"Really! You had a vision? I don't ever remember you having one before."

"That's because I don't believe that I ever did. When he took me into a vision, I seen the most beautiful garden that I ever saw in my entire life. There were flowers out of this world, the colors were prettier than I have ever seen. I seen stones, that stood out to me that were laid out all over to walk on in the garden. I seen butterflies that were amazing. God said to me that this is the beauty that he is going to take April, even as she is still a young child. He said that our family will be used by him in a great way. That healing and forgiveness will be there for all of us. Oh, Karen it was incredible what I seen and heard God say to me."

"God told you that healing was coming and he was going to use our little girl even though she is still young?"

He seen tears in his wife's eyes. "Yes, he did." He reached over and held onto her hand. "He told me that I need to pray for the lost, not wish death on them no matter what they had done."

"I'm so thankful God showed you that and gave you that word." She looked at April, and seen she wasn't even paying any attention, she was busy coloring on the children's menu.

The waitress came back with their food. "Can I get anything else for you?" she asked sitting their food down in front of them.

"No thank you, this looks delicious."

"Thank you, enjoy your meal."

"I love the coffee here, its better than what we drink at home." Karen commented.

"I don't know if it's really better, or if its just because we haven't had any in so many hours." Micah chuckled. "Let's bless the food."

"Amen." April said after her father finished up the prayer.

The three started on eating their food. They all felt so hungry, and they knew they still had a long drive before getting home. "I'm glad we stopped here to eat, I think the food is great, and the price is not so bad either." Karen spoke.

"I'm enjoying my fish that's for sure."

"I like my hot dog too, and French fries." April said taking another bite of her hotdog.

They finished up their food and drinks and made sure to use the restroom before heading out for the long drive back home.

"Well according too the app map, we still have another six hours left for driving. We should get home by ten o'clock."

April laid down in the back seat, she felt so tired because she had to get up so early for the long drive to come to court.

Karen felt tired herself, she laid her head back on the head rest, and she quickly fell to sleep. Leaving Micah up all alone to drive in peace and quiet. Here he decided to take the time to talk to God again.

13

Morning came and Karen got up to make breakfast for Micah before he headed out to work. Jimmy was out of school for the summer and now it was his turn to sleep in.

"Micah, how was your night?" she asked seeing him sitting in quietness drinking his coffee while waiting for his breakfast.

"It was good, how was yours?"

"I had a dream I wanted to share with you."

"Okay, go ahead." "Now I don't know if this has anything to do with what the vision you told me that you had. But I had a dream that April was so happy, and helping other children that was sex trafficked like she was."

"Really! I know that God is about to do something. After what he showed me, I know that he is going too."

"So, you think that I should take that dream was from the Lord?" She handed him his breakfast, and watched him devour it so fast.

"I would, it was a good dream, and I believe God was wanting to show you something too."

"Thanks for the breakfast." He gave her a little kiss. "I love you honey, and thank you, for putting up with me. See you after work, have a good day."

"I love you too, have a good day honey."

It was still early, and she wanted to spend sometime in prayer while the children were still sleeping. She knelt down by her couch, giving God all glory and praise for what he was about to do in their lives. She knew that God is going to help her little girl get past all the trauma she had gone through, to where she was able to help other children. She cried to God with a thankful heart. After what April and her family had gone through over the last two years, it's a wonder they are even sane.

She decided to go and check on the children after she was done praying, to her amazement, April was not in her brother's room. She went to April's room and found her fast to sleep in her own bed. She looked like an angel laying there so peacefully. She smiled as she stood in the doorway watching her. Just another reason to be thankful, she didn't believe that her brother kicked her out of his room, but that she just decided that it was time to sleep in her own room. Then the thought came to her, *"that's right, we had court yesterday, now she knew those men went to prison, now she feels safe enough to sleep in her own bed."* She smiled again and walked back down stairs to start on house work.

Karen had always been neat and tidy, with the smell of sweetness aroma throughout her home. She loved to have plenty of plugins in the electrical sockets. She made sure to keep up on every little thing in her home. She knew that her husband worked very hard to support the family, and she had always felt that it was her duty as his wife to have her home looking good for the family.

As she cleaned, she sang keeping a joyful heart. It made her time a happy time although she was cleaning. She knew at one time she had almost forgotten how to clean her home. If was after April was kidnapped. She had given up on life for the most part, only hanging on enough for her son and husband.

Once she accepted Jesus Christ in her heart, things began to change for her, even though April was not yet home. But she finally had hope, after losing all hope when her little girl was no longer at home, and she didn't know where she was at. Today she has a reason to sing, although most would never sing while cleaning. Her daughter was home, her daughter is sleeping in her own bed at night, and never woke up screaming in torment. Yes, she has a lot to be thankful for.

She felt an excitement go all through her, although she was unsure of the feeling she was having. Where did it come from, and why was it there? She went about cleaning, waiting for April to get up, when her sister Rose called her up. "Good morning, Rose."

"Good morning, I wanted to apologize for leaving right when you got home last night. I was tired and wanted to sleep in my own bed, I hope you didn't mind."

"No, not at all. I am so thankful that you stayed with Jimmy all day again. I was tired last night too, after the day in court and long drive home."

"How did court go yesterday? I was praying that those men would spend the rest of their life behind bars, after what they had done."

"Court was very intense at first, when April got on the stand. Her father went crazy after hearing her tell of some of the things they had done to her."

"Oh, no really? Like what sort of things?"

Karen looked to make sure that April or Jimmy was not up yet before talking about it. "She was telling about them beating her so bad, that it nearly killed her."

"Oh, my sweet Jesus, those evil people do that heinous crime to little children, they need someone to take a ball bat to their heads. Maybe than they will think of the evil they are doing to little children." She was so angry after hearing her niece was beat almost at the point of death.

"Micah couldn't handle hearing that and about her being raped by different men. He stood up and started to scream and yell at the men. The judge ended up having him escorted out of the courtroom."

"Wow, yeah, I can't blame Micah for feeling outraged like that, I would have done the same, maybe even worse. Knowing me and my temper when I get upset, I might have walked right up to them and started punching them."

"Oh, trust me, I wanted to do that and a whole lot more."

"I can't understand how you were able to sit through that hearing knowing what happened to your daughter."

"It wasn't easy at all. But I made her a promise, that I would not leave her alone in the courtroom. There were so many times I felt like I was going to throw up. My stomach got so sick, I had to pray and ask God to help me so I didn't run out and leave her alone. She kept looking back to make sure I was still there."

"Yeah, I don't know if I could have done that."

"When it's your child that is suffering, you would do anything for them, and that means putting aside your own feeling about things and do what is best for them. April needed me there, I had to overcome my own thoughts, and know that it was her that went through it, if she could survive that evil that was done to her, then I can overcome hearing what she went through. How can I be of any kind of help, if I'm not strong enough for her to talk with me about it."

"Just think there are still so many little children going through this garbage every day. Evil men still raping the children, still killing them. I think God is going to do something to put an end to such things. These sweet little children are forced to do this sick stuff on a daily basis, and they can't run from it, they would only be caught trying, then I'm sure beaten for trying to run away."

"There was a lot that April never even told me about what happened to her, until she was on the stand."

"Really! Like what kind of stuff, I thought that she told you everything."

"I thought so too, but no not even close."

"I wondered why she waited until she got to court before talking about it."

"I think maybe because she was trying not to think about it, because they were so bad."

"What sort of things did she say."

"After Micah left the courtroom, more things come out like, there were times that two men came in to rape her at the same time, they took turns. Some did her in the butt, some made her have oral sex with them."

"Oh, my gosh, those evil men, how can they even be called men, they are animals."

"I'm just thankful that Micah was already out of the room."

"Did you end up telling him about that?"

"No, I just can't, I mean if you would have seen the rage in him. He scared me to pieces by how crazy he got."

"He did all of that in court?"

"No, there were a lot of the news media outside of the court house, just waiting on the steps to talk to who ever will give them their time. Well Micah did after court, he wouldn't speak to them before court, but after court, he was like a person I didn't even know. He started to say on camera, they needed to bring hanging back, and he would personally hang every man in the court house."

"Oh wow! Are you kidding me?"

"It was very bad. But on our way home, God took him into a vision, he showed him the most amazing garden."

"Really, a vision of a garden, so what does that all mean?"

Karen filled every detail in for her sister, the two continued to talk until she heard the kids coming down the stairs. "I need to get going, my babies are up now." She never wanted them to hear her talking about what happened in court.

"Okay, hang in there things will get better, you have the promise of God now."

"Yes, I do, we shall chat later bye." She looked at her children. "Good morning my beautiful children." She felt happy knowing that God was going to do some amazing things, in his timing. She just had to trust him, because he knows just what needs to be done.

"Morning mama." They both said.

"Are you hungry?"

They talked for a few minutes, then she started to cook them some pancakes.

"Kids, your pancakes are done, come and eat." She yelled for them. She was hoping that April would say something to her about sleeping in her own bed. She didn't want to tell her that she checked in on her and noticed that she did.

April and Jimmy walked into the kitchen. "Yum, I love to eat pancakes mama. I missed them when I wasn't here." Her voice drifted off to a silence.

"Well, my sweet girl, you can have them everyday here if you like. You are no longer there, so we will think of the good things, okay?"

April put a smile on her face. "Okay mama, the good things."

Karen went to walk away, to start to clean up the little mess she made, while making pancakes, when April started to talk again.

"Guess what mama." She spoke excited.

"What baby."

"I slept in my own bed last night. Didn't I Jimmy?"

"Yep."

"Wow! You slept in your own bed, I'm so proud of you honey. Did you wake up scared at all?"

"Nope, not last night, I think because we went to court, and I know that the guys went to prison and can't get out to come and get me." Her mother was so happy knowing that April felt peace now enough to sleep in her own bed.

"Honey, it's only going to get better from here on out. We will still have you go and see Mrs. Walker for now, until you know that you know longer need to see her, how does that sound?"

"Yes mama, I like her. I think she has helped me a lot."

"I think so too honey, I like her also. So, what do you kids want to do today?" she asked changing the subject.

"Can we go swimming in the pool?"

"Sure, you can." She smiled at April, knowing that for two long years, she had missed out on so many good things. She was happy to see her daughter coming out of her shell, so-to-speak. She wondered for a while there if she was ever going to get better, for the first month and a half when she first came home. She was such an emotional wreck, it scared Karen for her daughter's life. Screaming and crying and keeping a distance from everyone, feeling like everyone was out to hurt her.

Karen decided that she was going to be making a cake today. She hadn't made anything like that it a couple of weeks, now that the children were ready to go outside and go swimming, she had the kitchen to herself to sing while baking. She no sooner pulled out a large bowl from her cupboard, her phone started to ring. Picking up her phone, she noticed it was her husband calling her. "Hi honey, is everything alright?" she wasn't used of Micah calling her in the morning hours, unless it was of very importance.

"You would not believe who I just got a phone call from."

"Who?" she could hear excitement in his voice.

"Do you remember that man that approached us when we came out of the courtroom?"

"Which one, there were several of them coming up to us." She remembered seeing a mob of people asking them questions.

"The last one, he handed me his card, then I gave him mine."

"Oh, yes, I remember now. What about him?"

"He just called me, and he said that he would love for me or you and April to go on tv, and give an interview about what happens when children are kidnapped and forced into sex trafficking."

"Wow, that didn't take him long to get ahold of you. But I don't think that we should do that." She spoke.

"Honey, why not? Look who we can help out by doing that. I think that this is part of what God was telling me that he was going to use April to help others even at her young age. I mean of course I wouldn't want to force her into doing anything that she would not feel comfortable into doing. But I just feel very good about this. I don't think people even realize just how bad it has gotten out there with the children being sold into sex slavery. I think its our duty to let the world know what we had went through. Better yet what our daughter had gone through, and what happens to the children that are brought back home."

She could hear the passion in him as he spoke about telling the world about their experience. As she heard him talking, she remembered her dream also. "I think you make a great point, I will talk with April today, and see how she feels about it. I will either let you know tonight when you come home, or I will call you back."

"Honey, is April busy right now, this man wants to know, because he said the interviews get filled fast, and he has others that would come on for other reasons. So, I asked him to give me a few minutes."

"Her and Jimmy are swimming right now, but I will go out there to ask her what she feels like doing."

"Wow it's still early and they're already swimming?"

"They just went out there after eating their breakfast. Let me call you right back."

"Okay, you might want to let her know that this can help a lot of people."

"I'll do my best honey." She rolled her eyes; she was not wanting to put any pressure on her at all. She wanted it to be something April wanted to do all on her own, without talking her into it. She hung the phone up and walked out to the pool. "April, can I have a word with you for a minute honey."

April wondered if something was wrong, for her mother to come out to the pool, right after she got in it. "Did I do something wrong?" she questioned her mother.

"Oh, no honey not at all. Your father just called me, and I'm not sure if you can remember when we left the court room, but a man gave your dad a card, and then your dad gave him one of his."

"I remember."

"Honey, that man called your dad today, he was wondering, if you and I or you and your dad, would like to go on tv."

Her eyes got big, and Jimmy yelled out "go on tv why?"

"Why mama does he want me to go on tv?"

"Well honey, he would like for you to tell your story, you know about you being kidnapped and what the evil men do once they kidnap children."

April looked at her mother, then at her brother. "Will I be helping anyone mama?"

"Oh, honey I believe that it will help a lot of people out. I think the more the story is told, is all the more people it will help."

"Then I will do it. I hate them hurting us kids, and I want them all to be caught."

"I do too honey, so it is okay for me to let your dad know that you are okay with going on tv and telling your story?"

"Yes mama." She gave a half smile. She was a kind sweet child, and would do anything to help children out. After what happened to her, and what she seen happen to others, she felt that if there was something she could do to help, then she would do that.

As Karen was walking back towards the house, she remembered that it was Wednesday and she needed to take April to go see her therapist, Ellie. She turned back around looking at April. "April, honey, I forgot all about today you go and see Mrs. Walker. You can swim for a few more minutes and you need to get dressed so I can take you there. After you come back home you and Jimmy can go swimming."

"Okay mama." She looked at Jimmy. "Well, we got to get wet for a few minutes." She chuckled.

Karen called her husband back right away. "She said yes she will do that, so go ahead and let the man know."

"That's great honey, was she okay with it, or did you talk her into it?"

"No, I would not have talked her into it. She asked me if it would help anyone, I told her that I believed that it would, so she said yes, she would do it."

"That's great, I'm going to call him right now."

"After you speak to him, let me know what he says."

"Okay, I'll call you back."

14

Micah called the man and got all the information about when they would be going on television. He was happy to know that they could bring to light the hidden things of darkness to the world or to those that wanted to listen.

"Hello." Karen answered.

"I called him, and he would like for you and I and April all to go on tv. He thinks by having both parents on with her, will make a bigger impact on people then only having one of us."

"So, when is that supposed to be?"

"He said in two weeks, he will call us before the time to make sure we are ready for it."

"Okay, that sounds great. I've never been on television before." She laughed.

"Neither have I, but this will be for a good cause, to get the evil exposed."

"Yes, that's true. Well honey enjoy your day, and I will see you at home tonight."

"Sounds like your busy."

"I have to take April to go and see Ellie, I had forgotten all about it, now I need to get her out of the water and get dressed."

"Okay, see you tonight honey."

Karen walked back outside after seeing that April hadn't come in the house yet. "April, April, it's time for you and Jimmy to come in the house. We don't want to be late getting you to the therapist. Come on the two of you."

"Okay mama, we are coming."

Karen left her baking things out on the counter, she knew that it was no big deal to do that, she would just make the cake once they were back home again.

"Okay, mama I will hurry and go get dressed." April said as she went around the corner and ran up the stairs.

Karen could hear the stairs thump as she ran up them, then followed close behind her was Jimmy to get out of his wet clothes and put dry ones on.

Karen grabbed her purse and waited for the children to come down the stairs. "Okay, we need to get going. Ellie will wonder where we are at."

"Can we go swimming again when we come home mama?"

"Sure you can, but you might be a little hungry when you get out of Ellie's."

"Maybe."

They went out to the car, and headed out of the driveway, when they noticed that a large truck was pulling into their driveway. "What is that truck here for?" Karen asked out loud.

"It has Fed X on the truck."

"I wonder why they are here; I didn't order anything."

She stopped her car and got out and walked to the man that was in the truck. "Can I help you; I don't believe that we ordered anything."

"I have a package here for a Miss April Davis."

"Really, I wonder who ordered her something? Can you take and put it in my house for me. I will go and unlock it."

"Sure, I can do that."

Karen unlocked the door. "Just set it anywhere inside, when I come home, I will see what it is."

"Okay ma'am." He sat it down on the inside. "Have a great day ma'am."

"Thank you, you do the same."

She rushed back to her car; she knew that she needed to get April to her appointment. "Okay Kids hold on tight; mama has to speed a little."

"Mama, don't speed, you don't need a ticket." Jimmy said looking in the front at his mother starting to go faster then she usually did.

"Oh, I'm not going to go that fast, just a little bit. I will watch to see if I see any police and I will slow down then." She felt like she was going to be late if she didn't rush just a little bit.

"Mama, is going to get a police man mad at her." Jimmy whispered to April. Shaking his head, while watching his mother.

Karen was going a tad over sixty, when she heard the sound of police sirens coming up behind her. "Oh, no. You have got to be kidding me. I didn't even see him anywhere."

"See I told ya." Jimmy said to his sister.

April watched to see what the police was going to do to her mother. She had no idea of what happens when someone gets pulled over. She never remembered seeing anyone get pulled over before.

"I'd like to see your registration, proof of insurance and your driver's license."

"How fast was I driving?"

"I clocked you going sixty-three, in a fifty-five-speed limit."

"I'm so sorry." She spoke getting out everything that he asked for. "I was running late for my daughters therapy appointment."

The policeman looked in the back at the children, when he noticed April. "Is this April Davis."

"Yes, sir, I really hate to be late."

What came next no one would have expected it. The officer gave her back all of her information. "Please get her to her appointment, just slow down please."

"Thank you very much." She took off again driving, this time she went under sixty miles an hour. She felt a little late is better than a ticket. She wondered how the officer had heard about her daughter, and then just to hand her back her things and not give her a ticket. "Thank you, Lord, that he never gave me a ticket." She spoke quietly, but loud enough that the children heard her.

"Mama, I didn't know if he was going to take you away from Jimmy and I."

"Oh no, honey, he would never have done that. I shouldn't have been going fast, I knew that it was wrong to do that. We are not supposed to drive faster then the law tells us too."

"I told April that you were going to get a ticket. I knew that they police were going to pull you over."

"They did pull me over, but I did not get a ticket."

"You almost did mama." He said.

"Yes, almost did. Here we are April, lets get you in there honey." She rushed the children into the building.

"Jimmy and I will be out here waiting for you when you're done."

"Okay mama." She smiled when she walked into the office.

Karen and Jimmy sat down in the waiting room. Karen let Jimmy play on her phone, while they waited.

Karen got thinking about the box that waited for April at home. She just could not imagine who ordered her something, and she be unaware of it.

She watched Jimmy playing a game on her phone. She smiled as she watched him laughing at what he was playing. Before she knew it, April walked out of the office and into the waiting room. Then she remembered where she seen the police officer from. When her daughter never came home from school, the day she was kidnapped, he was one of the officers that came to her home. She was very surprised that he remembered her from back then. *"He must have recognized my name, and heard that she was back home now from somewhere."* She thought.

"I'm done, can we go swimming now." April said excited.

"Great, I do believe there is a big package waiting for you when we get home."

"For me?" she put a huge smile on her face. "What is it mama?"

"I don't know honey, I guess we will see when we get home."

The three headed to the car. Karen was just as excited to see what was in the box as April was. She wanted to drive fast going home just so she could see what it was. But she knew she didn't need another policeman pulling her over again. What kind of excuse would she use next, rushing home to open a box. She didn't think that another policeman would let her get by with that."

Arriving to their home, without any more police officers pulling her over. She could hardly wait to see what April got in the huge box. "Come on April, I want to see what you got in the box."

She unlocked the door, and took another good look at the name on the box. "Yep, it says your name right here, so let me go and get a knife, to cut it opened. I don't think you will be able to remove all of that tape yourself. I never can whenever I get a package."

April stood there anxiously awaiting, for her mother to cut it open at the top so she could see what was inside. "Hurry mama, I want to see what I have."

"Okay honey, I'm almost done." She cut the top opened so they could look down inside. "Okay, now you can see what it is."

April looked inside after removing some plastic and Styrofoam. "I can't tell what it is mama, will you help me get it out?" she asked so anxious to see what she got waiting for her.

"Here let me cut down a side to make it easier. I will cut both of the sides." She cut both sides until the box laid opened and they could see everything in the box. She noticed a piece of paper inside, picking it up she could see what all of this was. "Wow, now who ordered you a kitchen set for your bedroom?"

April heard what she said. "I have my own kitchen set?" she started to pull the package out. "Who bought it for me mama?"

"I don't know honey, no one told me about it. Here let me help you with that." Karen took everything out of the box, and removed the large plastic bag it was wrapped up into. "Let me put the box on the porch to get it out of the way here." She did just that to give more room to see what she all got.

"Look mama, look at the stove, and I have a little refrigerator."

"I see that, its so nice honey. What else do you have?"

April got picking up other things that came in the box. "I have pots and pans, some dishes. Wow look mama, I have this." She held up her own little fake blender.

"This is very nice honey; I do believe that you wanted all of this stuff before. Do you like it April?"

"Oh yes mama, I do. I want to put it in my bedroom, can I?"

"Of course, you can, let all three of us carry things up to your room."

"Okay mama." She grabbed some smaller things, and Jimmy took some small things, they ran upstairs, with them.

Karen watched the excitement on April's face. She thought that this could help her get her little girl back the way it should have been all along. Picking up the stove, she carried it up to April's bedroom. "Okay now we need to put all of these things in a nice spot, somewhere where you will want to have your kitchen at."

"Can we put it by this wall mama, I don't have anything there but my laundry basket."

"Sure, we can honey, this way you can also look out your window."

"Mama, if you never bought me this, who did?"

"Oh, honey I am pretty sure that it came from your dad. He wants you to have everything that you wanted before. I'm sure he will be buying you a bike next of some kind." She smiled. "Just to be sure, I will call him up after we set up your kitchen."

April hugged her mother, she felt so happy, being home, knowing that the men that hurt her was all locked up for years. She was finally feeling safe in her home with her family. "I'm so happy mama." She shed some tears of joy. This also made Karen shed some too. Jimmy stood watching both his mom and sister hug and cry.

"Why are you guys crying?" He asked not understanding it.

"We are happy honey." Karen spoke giving him a smile.

"I thought that your supposed to cry when your sad, not when you're happy."

"Do you remember when daddy bought the pool? What did you do when you could start swimming in at your own home?"

He thought about it for a moment. "I cried."

"Okay, when you cried, were you happy you had a pool to swim in, or was you sad that we had a pool?"

"I was happy, I know now why your crying, it's because she got all of this stuff to play house with."

Karen laughed knowing that he understood a part of it. "Well let's get the rest of the things down stairs, and get this all set up."

"Okay mama." They took off back down stairs.

After everything was all set up, Karen wanted to call up her husband. But first she needed to tell April something. "April, you have a very nice easy bake oven here. This really will let you cook some cookies or cake in it." After she said the word cookie, Jimmy took notice in it right away.

"I thought that they are called happy rounds now."

"Its okay now mama, we can call them cookies."

Karen looked at April, "are you sure about that honey, I just simply made a mistake."

"It's okay we can call them cookies, that is their name and Mrs. Walker told me that I don't have to ever be afraid to hear the name cookies anymore."

"Oh, honey that is great. Here are some cake mixes that came with your easy bake oven. Maybe you and Jimmy will want to make some." That's when she remembered that she too was going to bake a cake. She had everything left out on the counter waiting to be put together. "Okay I am going down stairs and let you kids play, I want to call up your father and asked if this came from him."

"Okay, I think we will make some cake, then go swimming."

"You should eat some lunch soon, its past the time."

"Okay."

Karen needed to know if the gift was from Micah, who else would have bought such a gift for her."

15

It was nearly two weeks past, and time was getting close for them to have their interview on tv. Karen was a little nervous, all the while Micah could hardly stop talking about being on tv. April said that she wanted to help parents to know that there are bad people out there that will hurt their child, and not care what happens to them.

"Are you ready for tomorrow?" Micah asked both Karen and April. "The big day is already upon us, I have been praying that this will get people aware of the danger allowing children to run rampant. At any time, they can be kidnapped and sold into sex slavery." He looked at April after he said that. "I'm sorry baby, I just don't want it to happen to anyone else."

"I know daddy, and I don't either."

"We will say what we feel needs to be said when we speak." Micah said.

"Honey, I am quite sure they will be asking us the questions to answer."

"Well, maybe so, but I am sure when we answer what they ask, we will be able to tell the people how it was for us, otherwise, why would they want us to come on tv and talk about it."

"Well, that's true."

"I just want to get these evil people exposed. Like April said, there were even lawyers at that place raping the children." Micah commented.

"Daddy, I seen a judge there too."

Micah looked at his daughter. "But how did you know that he was a judge honey?"

"When he came into my room, he told me that he used to put men away that did this stuff. He said that he is a judge, but it became so common now, that there are so many, he wanted to see what it was all about."

"Oh my gosh, did he do anything to you honey?"

"Yes." She lowered her head remembering the words that he spoke to her and then what he did afterwards.

"What kind of a judge is that, he used to lock them up, then he decided to be a monster just like the ones he locked up. I'd like to see him somewhere; I'd rip his head off of him."

"Honey, remember what God showed you in the vision, we must remain calm through it all. If we are to help others then we need to remain calm. I understand the angry baby, but we must keep focus, to accomplish all that God has for us to do."

Micah looked at his wife, he knew what she was saying was true, God needed to show him things, and he needed to stay calm so God could use him. If he would rip off everyone's head for hating what they did, or stood for, there would not be to many people left. The people in the world have lost their minds, they are calling evil good, and good evil. Just what the bible speaks about. Karen was hoping that she would have the chance to say that while she was on tv, she thought that would be a good thing to let people ponder on. God knew ahead of time that there was going to be days like this, so he for warned us ahead of time.

"Let's stay focused, I think I smell food cooking." Micah put his thoughts together.

"Everyone have a seat; I will have supper right away. It's all done."

"April, I need you to please forgive me honey, for yelling again and getting so upset about those men."

"I forgive you daddy; I get mad too when I think about what they did to me and the other kids. I used to really hate them all so much. I wanted them to all die, but Mrs. Walker is helping me to forgive them. She told me that as long as I hang on to unforgiveness, that I will stay bitter, and she said the bible says that bitterness is like rottenness to the bones. She told me that when I can learn to forgive them for all they did, that I will start to feel safe and happy again."

He listened to his daughter. "I think that Mrs. Walker is a very wise woman. What she said is all true honey."

"Let's eat." Karen spoke.

"Daddy, I made you a cake from my oven you bought me."

"You did? Wow that's great honey."

"She's been cooking up a storm lately. Now that she has gotten the hang of things." Karen spoke.

"Me too, I help her cook mama."

"I'm sorry Jimmy, yes you do help your sister. And you are a big help to her."

He smiled, and looked at his dad. "I helped her make the cake for you daddy. We ate one earlier and then we gave one to mama, and made you one. But you can't have it until you eat your supper."

"Okay, well I better eat everything on my plate then so I can have a snack."

Everyone ate the meal that was set before them, some talked more then they ate, like Jimmy giving warning that his daddy will like the cake so much, he will want them to bake him another one.

"What does everyone think about after we eat, that we all go swimming" Micah said.

"That sounds fun, just as long as we don't eat too much. It will not feel so good swimming on a full belly."

"You heard your mother, don't eat to where you can't swim."

After they were done eating, all four of them got their swim suits on and went swimming. This was the first time that all four were in the pool together since April came home. They laughed and splashed each other for nearly two hours then it was time to come in for the evening. Micah knew that the following day was the big day, and he wanted everyone well rested.

After putting the children to bed, he and Karen laid in their bed talking for a while before drifting off to sleep.

Morning came with the light shining through the windows in their room. "Honey, we need to get up, get out showers and eat then drop off Jimmy at Rose's house and get going." Micah was happy the day had finally arrived for them to speak their mind on tv.

"Okay I'm getting up."

Waking the children to get up and get their showers also, the morning was being rushed to leave the house.

Arriving at a near by studio Mr. Chambers was there to meet the Davis's before they arrived.

"Okay we better get inside, do I look alright?" he asked his wife.

"Yes Micah, your worse than a woman, you already asked me that three times. Now come on let's get in there, you look good."

They walked inside the building being greeted by Mr. Chambers. "I'm glad to see that you all have made it, please come on in here. This is the place that we will be giving the live interview."

"Oh, I didn't know that it will be live." Micah spoke giving a smile. He would have told some people that he knew that he was going to be live, so they too could have watched it.

"Oh, I thought that I had mentioned that."

Karen hurried and made a quick phone call to her sister Rose to tell her to be watching.

"You can all take a seat right here, I'd like April to sit closest to me, so when I talk with her, she won't need to be leaning over you."

"Okay." They took their seats, then he took his.

"I will start out by introducing you to the people in their homes. Then I will mention about the topic we will be talking about. I will give each of you room to share some of your experience with what it was like for you going through this sort of thing." He focused his attention on to April. "Now April I know that this is about what happened to you, do you think that you will be able to answer my questions?"

"Yes."

"Okay let's get the lights on, and we will get started in a minute." He looked at the time, seeing that they only had a minute left before it was to start. "Before we get started, I just wanted to say, although we don't have a live audience, we will be accepting others to call in and talk."

Micah looked at Karen and shrugged his shoulders. "I didn't know that was going to happen."

They could hear a man's voice counting down, "5,4,3,2,1 you're on."

"Hello everyone, welcome to my show, The Jack Chambers show. I have a very important guest with me today. Her name is April Davis." He looked at April, while showing the people watching which one, she was. "This is her mother Karen, and her father Micah. We are going to be telling a story about child sex trafficking. A little over two years ago, April was a victim of this horrendous crime. I'm going to allow April to share with us what happened on the day she found herself caught up with men that did this to her. April, can you tell what happened to you on the day you were kidnapped?"

"I was walking home from school, when a man grabbed me and put me in his car."

"How old were you at the time this happened?"

"I was seven years old."

"When this man put you in his car, do you remember what happened to you after that?"

"He tied my hands up, and told me that from now on my name was Cookie."

"So, this man tied your hands up and then he started to call you by the name Cookie. What happened after that?"

"We drove for a long, long time. It got dark and I was scared of what he was going to do to me."

"Can you tell us, what happened next?"

"He took me to a big place, and made me go inside where it was stinky."

The man looked at her. "You said that it was stinky, like what do you mean?"

"My mom always had our home smell good; she puts things in the wall that makes it stay smelling nice. But that place stunk really bad, it made me feel sick to my stomach. I had to go to the bathroom really bad, and they never let me use the toilet and I stood there and wet my pants on the floor.

After that happened, the man that kidnapped me, slapped me really hard across my face."

"Wow, what did they end up doing to you after that?"

April took a deep breath. "They took me down a long hallway, I could hear kids crying, and they put me into a dirty dark room, that had no windows in there. The bed was really nasty, and it stunk very bad in there."

The man focused his attention on Karen. "Mom, can you tell me what it was like for you when your daughter didn't come home from school?"

Karen was telling about how she felt like she was going to die, how each day that went by without her daughter, she wanted to die, but knew she had a son to raise, and a husband that needed her too. She spoke on how she never was a church goer until April was kidnapped and how her new found faith in God helped her and her family, where it untimely brought April back home to them.

"That is so hard on the family after having a child not return home from school." Mr. Chambers spoke. "Micah, can you tell me what it was like for you as a father, to not have your daughter come home from school?"

"I felt useless, I wanted to die. I felt like I was no good anymore. I couldn't work, I couldn't love my family like they needed me too. I was empty, I had nothing in me to want to go on anymore. There was a time, I thought about taking my own life." He looked at his wife. "I never told her that until now."

"I think as a father myself to a little girl, I can understand that feeling, I probably would have felt the same way. So, what gave you the strength to keep going?"

"I believe it was like my wife said, after we started going to church, and learned to pray and had friends that prayed with us from our church we go too, God was able to bring healing to us. It was after we decided to start going to church and we gave our lives to Jesus, that's when our daughter was able to be found, within months. And she was brought back to us."

"That is incredible. Now April I'd like to ask you if your able to tell us, some of the things that happened to you when you were still at that place."

"I was raped a lot, and beaten up really bad."

"Who were the ones that beat you up? Were they the men that raped you, or the men that worked there?"

"They both did. Sometimes I would fight the men trying to keep them from raping me, and they would beat me. Sometimes Travis would beat me really bad, he even broke my arm once and my rib for kicking me there."

"Wow, so this man Travis, who was he?"

"He worked for Kevin, and Kevin would tell him to take care of me because I was fighting the men that wanted to rape me."

"Who was Kevin then?" he was confused.

"Kevin is the one that bought me from the man that kidnapped me."

"Oh, okay I got ya. Can you tell me anything else."

"I wanted to come home to my family. But they told me that it was my family that gave me to them. They told me that my family hated me and didn't want me anymore."

"Did you believe them?"

"No, not at first. But after I was there for so long, I kind of started to believe it, because my parents weren't coming to get me."

When Karen heard her tell that she started to believe it, she started to have tears come down her cheeks.

"Karen, I see you getting emotional, can you tell us what you're feeling right now?"

"I hurt because I know what they did to my daughter was just evil. Those grown men would come into her room and rape her fifty-sixty times a day. They made her feel so unloved and unwanted. What kind of a person can do such evil to little children that cannot defend themselves. I hurt for all the little children out there that have been abused, rather by kidnappers or a family member. We need more being done to protect the children, when we here about some of these perverts are lawyers and judges, it just makes me sick to think, these are the same men that we turn to for help, but they are the same ones that are raping our son's and our daughters."

"Are you telling me that there were judges and lawyers that had raped your daughter?"

"Yes, that is what I am saying. We only see the ones that have a building that are selling our children, we are not catching the ones that pay good money to rape our babies."

Micah decided to start talking without being asked. "It's just like what happened at Jeffrey Epstein, he had that sort of thing going on at his place for years. But there he also had gown women being used and raped. There were documents showing little children were there being raped by big men. When I say big men, I'm talking about the judges and lawyers there were doctors. It's become the highest paying industry. People pay billions of dollars a year to rape children and many of these children die from their injuries."

"April, when you were in that place, did you ever see anyone else there that was raped, or maybe even killed?"

"Yes, lots of them being raped. I seen some little boys where they were bleeding from their butts."

"Oh wow, okay let's talk about the deaths you said that you knew of. What happened?"

"I seen a girl that was across the hall from me, being carried out by two men after they raped her. She was screaming and going crazy when they were hurting her, then all of a sudden it got very quiet there, so I looked out my curtain, and I seen her body was not moving, and two guys carried her out, and I never seen her again. I also seen where a little boy was bleeding bad after he was raped, and he too was carried out later. I never seen him again either."

The man spoke with them for a while longer but then their time was up. "I really appreciate you all taking the time to come here today. Sorry I decided since the topic was so strong, that we would not be taking any calls. But I'd like to invite you all again and we can continue to discuss more if you're willing to come back."

Micah looked at April and Karen. "What do you think?"

"Yes, I think that would be ok."

"Great I will call you up when we will be ready for that." He shook Micah's hand. "I will be sending over a copy of todays show to your home."

"That's great. Thank you, for having us come on here."

"We will talk real soon, be safe."

16

On their way home. Micah was thinking about the interview they just had. "How do you think that it went today?"

"I think it was okay, I like the fact that he wants us to come back again."

"Maybe next time we go on, I will be able to say a little more."

"I thought that you were going to today, what happened with that?"

"I'm not to sure, maybe I got a little chocked up." He said.

"You getting chocked up, I doubt that honey. You usually have a mouth full to say, and you don't care who hears it."

"Well, then I don't know what happened. But I still think that it went good for us speaking on tv for the first time about what happened."

"I do too." Karen looked in the back at April. She was sound to sleep. "Awe, look, she is sleeping, I was wondering why she was so quiet back there."

"Maybe what she spoke about today, brought back some very bad memories, and maybe sleeping is one way to block them out."

"I don't know so much about that, look when she first came home for nearly a month every night, she woke up screaming, having terrible nightmares about being there still."

"Thank God, she isn't doing that anymore. She's been home for three months now, and she is still going through some rough patches."

"Honey, when something like that happens to the children, many of them never get better, some of them have a strong mind set on getting better so they do whatever they can to be healed from the trauma they gone through. I read some stories, where some children that had been raped over and over like April, and abused badly, never recover. They are wounded for life."

"All because evil hearted people chose to take their innocent lives and kill the inside of them from any dreams they might have had. These men, I can't say are beyond saving, because God is merciful, and his love is so much more then we can ever have I believe until we get to heaven. But I believe most of then never want to be healed, they like the evil that they are doing to children. See it's a good thing that I am not God, I would have killed everyone of them by now to save the children. But God and his mercy has not done that."

Karen chuckled the way her husband said if he were God, he would have killed them all by now. "I wonder what God thinks when he hears his children talk about killing other human beings for the wrong they do. The bible tells us that we all have come short from the glory of God."

"Oh, honey I know that, but if you just think about it for a minute, if these evil people would all die, then the children would never have to be raped and tortured."

"I understand that, but what I think of if every man that went to rape the children, would lose his private parts, then his hands break to where he couldn't hurt them. And for the ones that are doing the kidnapping, if their legs would break so he couldn't grab a child, that would start eliminating our children from getting hurt by them."

"Hahaha! You make me laugh, lose his private parts, if it was that simple. I guess we can always dream of that happening to them."

"I wonder when we will hear back from his again? I wonder why he decided not to take live phone calls?"

"I think he said because of the topic that we were talking about. I'm glad he didn't take any, because who knows what kind of jerk might have called in saying something stupid. I wouldn't want to go off shouting on tv for everyone to hear me when I get angry."

"Yeah, I'm glad he didn't have that too. I'm happy that it was just him asking the questions, and he seems to be a pretty decent guy."

"Yeah, like he said, he has a little girl too, and he would have gone nuts if something like that happened to her."

"I wonder if Rose watched us?"

"Oh, I don't know. I wish that I would have known that it was going to be live, I would have told several people to watch us."

"Me too. I would have told my parents to watch it."

"I'm just glad that it's over with now, so now I can concentrate on my work more. I was so focused that we were going to be going on tv, I wasn't paying attention to anything."

"I know, that's just about all you talked about."

After picking Jimmy up at Roses house, they went home to getting a meal all ready to eat and relax for the rest of the day.

The following day when Micah was at work, he received another phone call from Jack Chambers. "Hello Micah, this is Jack Chambers, I hope you remember me."

"I sure do, wasn't I just on your tv show yesterday." He laughed.

"You sure was, I just wanted to let you know what happened after the show."

"Okay, what?" Micah was curious to know what happened.

"Our phones began to light up like crazy. The people went crazy over watching you and your family, and they all want you back. They were saying people need to be made more aware of what is happening to the children when we hear about them being kidnapped. Many families never get to see their child again. Many children end up dead, like your daughter spoke about her seeing some being carried out that had died."

"Wow, that's great. Sure, we can come back and speak more about it."

"I was talking with my producer, and he was telling me that it might be a good idea, to have it where people can call in and ask you questions. How do you feel about having it like that this next time?"

Micah thought how he could word it to him how he felt about it. "My wife and I both agreed that it was probably a good thing that you didn't have it that way."

"Can I ask you why you feel that way?"

"Well, what is some jerk was to call in and say something stupid to my daughter who has already been through so much. What if they called her a liar, or I don't know for sure, maybe something that would really hurt us as a family that has already been so hurt."

"I hear ya, and yeah, I can't blame you for feeling like that. What is we screen them first; you know find out what question they would be asking first being its live? Do you think that might change your mind about it?"

"I think that would work, I mean I have to protect my family from people being haters or just rude."

"Okay I will talk with my producer about that, and see what we can do. After I speak with him about it, I will give you a call back."

"Do you know when I should be excepting to hear back from you?"

"I think later today, if that works for you."

"Oh sure, that's fine."

After they hung up, Micah called Karen up right away. "Guess what honey." He was excited.

"Humm, I don't know, what?"

Mr. Chambers called me just a few minutes ago."

"Really, already?"

"He told me that after the show was over, the lights in the place went crazy. People were calling in telling him they want us back on to talk more about what happened and what its like to go through that sort of thing. They were saying how people need to be made more aware of this so people will protect their children more from this happening."

"Wow, well that's great. I think people need to know more about it too."

"There is one thing though, I'm not sure how you will feel about it."

"What's that?"

"He said that his producers would like to make it where people can call in and ask questions."

The two stayed on the phone talking for a while, Micah filled in everything that he and Mr. Chambers had spoken about.

"I say then let's do it that way, if they agree to screen the calls first."

After hanging up the call, Karen decided to pray about the matter. She looked at her children playing outside on the swings, all the while she was walking around in her home praying. "Father God, you know I want to do what is best to help other people. I know the dream that you gave me and the vision you gave to Micah. Lord, you said that you were going to use my April to help others. Is this a start by us going on tv to tell her story, our story? I want to do what is right by my daughter, and I don't want others to ever hurt her again. Lord, not with their words or their actions. So please just show us what your will is for us, in Jesus' name amen." She stood at the window watching April and Jimmy, she could slightly hear the laughter coming from the both of them. Tears dripped down her cheeks as she was thinking that just a few months ago, she was begging God to bring her daughter home to her. Now she was home, and she could not imagine anyone ever hurting her again. She was now keeping a close eye on the both of her children. She didn't want to live in fear that something was always right there to hurt her children, but she didn't want to be stupid either by thinking everyone was good.

She knew first hand now, that children can be taken at any moment when they are unprotected. She refused to allow her children to run up and down the sidewalks now, without her or her husband being right there to watch them. They were no longer allowed to go to the near by park, to play unless she was right there with them.

Many things had changed in their lives after April being kidnapped. It hasn't always been easy to make such changes, and at times it seemed to be uncomfortable. Like the times that Jimmy wanted to ride his little bike down the sidewalks, not always did Karen feel like going with him so he could ride, but she knew that it would be far better for her to be a little uncomfortable then to have her child kidnapped. That was a nightmare, it almost claimed her life when April didn't come home for two years. She didn't know for the longest time if her daughter was still alive or not.

She had to learn the hard way about watching the children much better than she did before. If she could get the warning out to the parents, so they would never have to go through what she did, then that's what she needed to do. She decided to call her husband back up.

"Hello Karen." He seen that it was her calling him. "What's up?"

"I've been praying and doing a lot of thinking. I feel that it would be okay to have callers call in and ask us questions when we are live on tv."

"Really, what made you change your mind?"

"Honey, in life there are always going to be haters, and people that just don't think before they speak. But its up to us to warn others of the danger of allowing children to just run rampant. Honey, it really doesn't matter what others say, even if they do get rude and say things that we don't like. It's up to us to sound the alarm of what is going on, and what we as parents can do to protect our children."

"Okay, when he calls back, I will be sure to let him know that we are okay with having callers."

"Great, let me know when he calls you back. Is he supposed to be calling you back today?"

"Yes, he said after he talks with his producer."

"Okay good, just let me know right away okay. Because this time, we know that it will be live, and we will be able to tell others about it."

"Yes, that's a good idea. I'll call you back after I hear from him."

Karen went about getting stuff ready for a nice supper. She would look outside at the children to make sure all was well. She felt it was her job to keep a close eye on them, although she couldn't see anyway someone could possibly get in her back yard, without coming through the house to do so. Her husband had made it so safe that no one would even be able to climb over the fence to get in the back yard. She knew that he had spent thousands of dollars to get the fence in like it was. After April came up missing, Micah went crazy, as well as she just about lost her mind. Micah knew that his back yard was going to be a safe haven for his son, and his daughter if she would ever return. Now that she has, they had a back yard that even they couldn't get in the back unless they came through the house.

Waiting to hear back from Micah Karen tried to think of what she could say to the callers. Or just say to the people that would be watching them live on tv. She wanted to make sure that parents were aware of the danger of their child being kidnapped. She had been watching video's where men would try and rip the child out of the parent's arms, all the while the parents were hanging on their child fighting the kidnapper with everything they had. It was heart breaking to watch, but she wanted to know just what to look for.

Some of the video's she watched caused her to break down crying for the parents that could not hold on tight enough to their child, as a big strong man would shove the woman to the ground, and he take their child and ran to his car with them. She knew the hell she went through after April was taken in broad daylight. Even where others could have been walking at the time, just like that man that tried to kidnap that little girl at the school. He wasn't looking to see who was around, he was just grabbing a child, he didn't care who was around him.

Karen thought about that time, many times, and she was hoping that she would remember to talk about it while she was on tv, just to let people know that it can happen anywhere, and anytime of day or night.

There were times that she would see little children out playing all by themselves, knowing that at any time a wicked person can come along and grab that child. She would cringe at the thoughts of that happening to anyone she knows.

Her sister was telling her about when her and her husband went on a vacation, they seen several little children all dressed up looking so pretty and nice, getting their pictures taken. She said that it reminded her about how some of the women that kidnap the children will say that she is from a certain agency and would like to have the child be in a magazine modeling clothing. Then the parents trust the person, just to find out she was a person that would sell their child, and they never see their child again. Karen had such a passion to let people know what is going on in every state and in many towns around them. It has gotten so much worse than it has ever been before. She remembered a time that she would hear about some child being kidnapped and they were found dead in a field. That was terrible enough to hear of that happening once in a while. But now everywhere you look you hear about another child, and many children being kidnapped and sold into sex slavery.

She watched some video's where others had hidden camera's and they were videoing children with their hands tied and their mouths with tape over them, laying all over on the ground, beaten raped and some killed. Men were standing by the children selling them to others like they were cattle in line for the slaughter. Her heart broke to see such things happening all over the place. Many of the children are sold and sent to other countries, and never seen again. She knew that she had to do her part in bringing the darkness to light. To many people wanted to cover up what was being done to the children. Either they were all for raping children, or they wanted the money that comes from selling them.

The more video's she watched was all the more she knew that she needed to take a stand in fighting for the safety of the children, and make parents more aware that child sex trafficking was happening all over the place.

Even the stories that her daughter had told her and what she told during court, made her sick to her stomach. She wondered what could have happened that would cause a child to grow up to want to hurt children in such an evil way. Was it all about the money they were paid for each child every time someone had sex with them. Had money become their god, where they no longer had a conscience of right or wrong. Or was it the simple fact that children could not fight them off to protect themselves, so with that being said, they had power over the child. That alone must have given them some kind of satisfaction knowing that can control little children and do with them anything they wanted.

Karen started to write things down so she could read over them and pick out what she wanted to say on tv. The phone rang right when she was getting to what seemed to be a good thing to bring up to the people. "Hello honey."

"I just heard back from Mr. Chambers. He said that his producer doesn't feel the need to have the callers screened. I told him what you said that it didn't matter, because we will just have to let people know the truth no matter what people say."

"Okay, and what did he say?"

"Well, he would like us back on again, next Tuesday. 1 week from yesterdays, show."

"Okay, well I think that's a good thing. Maybe we will be able to say more things then yesterday."

"I think so too, otherwise why would he have us come back on again."

"Well, I've been writing things down, some of it I want to address to people watching us. It needs to be said so I want to have a chance to do just that."

"Honey, I've also been thinking."

"Like what honey?"

April heard the kids come into the house, she seen they were all wet. "Go change out of your wet clothes please."

"I've been thinking, I really think that the show should be with you and April honey, not me."

"Micah why are you saying that? I thought you liked the whole idea of going on tv. Did Mr. Chamber say something to you?"

"No, not at all honey, it's just me. Like yesterday, I hardly said anything, it was mostly you and April doing the talking, and I just really think that this is more down you and her ally. I'd rather focus on my work here at the office and let you two, help others with understanding the importance of protecting the children."

"Are you sure that's what is really going on?"

"Of course, I'm sure. I have no other reason, but just feel that this is something for the two of you to do."

"Have you spoke with Mr. Chambers about it?"

"No, but I'm going to call him up and talk with him about it."

"Okay honey, if that is how you feel, April and I can do this together then. I just know the more I watch the videos of the little children being kidnapped and sold for sex, is all the more I feel to expose the hidden darkness, and bring it to light."

"Well, there you go, its up to the two of you now. I love you honey, and I know that you two will do great. I'll see you tonight after work."

17

Karen had a lot that she wanted to say on the talk show. She had a list of things and would take that list with her. April knew that she would be questioned more, and possibly by people that would call into the show.

"April, remember what I said about everyone might not be nice when they call in. There maybe some that are quite rude. Some might try to hurt your feelings, are you sure that you are up to doing this?" she never wanted to force her into anything, she wanted it to be what she wanted to do.

"Yes mama, I know not everyone is nice, and I know that there may be some that are rude to me and to you."

"Okay, just so you understand what you're getting into, I know and I believe that you and I together will be able to help others out there, and maybe save the lives of other children. And maybe even to some that have been kidnapped and gone through much of what you have."

"Oh, mama, I wish I could help them. I know how evil having that done to you is. I can understand what they feel."

"I am so thankful to God that he has helped you so much. When you first came home, I was so scared for you. You crying all the time, you being afraid to talk to any of us. But look at you today honey, you are doing wonderful."

"I know mama, at times you might get upset with the way that I am, but I also know that it's not really my fault, and I am doing better now."

"I never get upset with you; I get upset with what has happened to you, that causes you to lash out at times, or stop talking to us. But for the most part, that is all behind us, and you are doing great."

"I just don't want to cry when I'm on tv. I want to be strong like you are mama."

"You listen to me April, you are stronger than anyone that I know. You have every reason to want to cry, and if you did while being on tv, then that is alright too. You must be yourself honey, no one can blame you for tears. Most of us have never gone through near the things that you have. And we think our problem is a lot, it's nothing compared to what you had. You have any idea of how much I look at you and think, that is one tough little girl. Look at her, hold her head high, and spend time with her little brother, watching over him so close so that no one hurts him."

April listened to her mother, tears fell to the floor, then she wrapped her arms around her mother. "I love you mama, I used to dream about what you smelled like. I remembered how you always had the house smelling so good. That used to keep me going and fighting to stay alive, so that one day I could smell you and the house again."

Karen could not believe what she was hearing. "Wow really, you remembered how I smelled?"

"Yes mama. That place there smelled really bad, I hated it from the first time I walked inside, well I never really walked, I was drug by a rope tied to my hands."

When Karen heard her daughter talk about her hands being tied up by a rope, it sickened her to the pit of her stomach. She hated to hear the evil that April had gone through, but she knew that she also needed to allow her to talk about it whenever she felt like she needed too. Also knowing this sort of thing, would help her have a better understanding of what to share with other people that didn't know about it.

"When do we go back on tv mama?"

"In two days, but this time your dad will not be coming with us. He is leaving that for you and I to be able to do."

"Why?"

"He feels like that it something that you and I should be doing together, and he stay at his job and work."

"Do you like it that way mama?"

"I think so, I know that God wants to use you and I to help others anyway that we can."

"Okay mama, it will be you and I. But what about Jimmy?"

"No, it's not for Jimmy honey, he would not understand any of this."

"Mama, I seen lots of boys Jimmy's age and even younger there getting raped."

Karen wanted to scream hearing that about the little children. She could only imagine the pain they were going through, from evil man raping them. She could not imagine having someone do that to her let alone a small child, and being a boy, she felt like it made it that much worse. She knew where they were going with them, and the pain that it had to of caused them. She didn't know if April even understood when a boy was raped just where it was at. She was only nine years old, and had seen and been through way too much, but still didn't know if she understood the difference between a boy a girl when it came time for having sex where it was done at. "Jimmy will stay with you aunt Rose while we go down to the studio."

"Okay mama." She got quiet like she was thinking. "Mama."

"Yes honey."

"Do you think that I could tell people about the boys that were raped there and would bleed from their butts?"

Karen was surprised she wanted to address that to people. "Well, I'm not sure if they will be allowed to tell on national television. Wait I think that you did mention something about it last time."

"Why not mama, that is what I seen happen. They made the boys bend over and did that to them in their butts." She spoke like she never even heard a word her mother said.

Karen knew now that she did understand there was a difference, and she hated the thoughts that those wicked men made her watch what they did to some of the boys. What kind of a monster would do such things to harm God's little children. It angered her to her very soul that such evil lies within man's heart. "Jimmy has not gone through any of that stuff, honey I really hope that you don't talk to Jimmy about any of this."

"No mama, I don't. I don't want to hurt him."

"Good, because he is just too young to understand any of it."

"I know."

Later on, after Micah came home, Karen waited until she put the children to bed, to talk with him about some things.

"Okay my dear, I know that something is on your mind. What is bothering you?"

"Today April and I were talking, some things I was not sure about, until we got talking. I don't know if you are aware about just what our little girl knows."

"Okay, like what are you talking about. I'm sure there are a lot of things she knows that we are not aware of."

"Honey, I don't know if I should even tell you what she told me today."

"Well, you might as just as well. I am her father and I think maybe I need to know more."

"She told me today, that the men at that place forced her to watch little boys get raped in their butts." She could see the look on his face after telling him.

"Oh my gosh, what kind of human would do that to little children. That could mess with a child's mind forever. Just to think what it's doing to the little boys."

"I could not believe it, I know that she told me before, that she seen a little boy bleeding from his butt, and then that little boy was carried out by two men."

"Yeah, but that wasn't telling you why he was bleeding from his butt."

"I know, now she asked me if she can talk about that on tv."

Micah could not believe that she wanted to do that. "Why did she ask you that?"

"She said because people to need to know what happens with the boys when they are kidnapped and sold into sex slavery. She had already mentioned it before, last week."

"Wow, she is absolutely amazing, how she wants to help people out, to get them to understand what is really going on. I mean she is only nine years old and wants to help out others so much. After everything she has gone through, she still looks to help others."

Karen smiled, she was so proud of April, she knew that she has a kind heart, and wants to help others out that has gone through things like she herself has. "She's a very sweet child, even before she was taken from us, she was always sweet. I'm so thankful that after all she's been through, she never lost that caring part of who she is."

"I can see that too; I thank God for that. Are you both ready to go on the talk show tomorrow?"

"I'm pretty sure that we are, I do need to ask April to word some things differently once she on tv then how she did with me."

"Oh, like what?"

"I was telling you what she told me about them making her watch boys get raped. Well, she wants to tell them on tv about their butts bleeding. I need her to tell it in a different way than that."

"Yes, I'd think so too. But her being so young, she doesn't fully understand all of that."

"I'm headed to bed, I feel tired, and I hate to go on tv looking all stressed and tired." She smiled at Micah. "Are you coming?"

"Yep, let me just make sure that all doors are locked up tight."

Karen laid in bed thinking about how to direct her talk to April in the morning about changing her words. She hated it to be so graphicly done on television. Future more she was not sure if it would be okay to speak it on the talk show. She remembered how Jack hurried and changed the subject last time.

Morning came and Karen was up asking April to get her shower. She went down stairs to start making her husband breakfast. "Thank you honey for making the coffee." She spoke seeing that Micah was already up having a cup of coffee.

"If I knew how to cook, I'd made us both breakfast, but I think you would rather have had dirt then my cooking." He laughed.

"Oh, come on you cook meat on the grill. It's not much different that that. But it's okay, I enjoy cooking." She pulled out a pan to start cooking some bacon.

"Are you all ready for today?" he asked looking at her, seeing that she still looked tired.

"I think so, although I had a rough night."

"Why?"

"I think I was just thinking to much, one thing you won't be with us today, so it's just her and me, I think I was feeling a little nervous."

"I'm sorry honey, I just felt like it was not what I am supposed to be doing. This is something that I believe God has for the two of you."

"It's okay, I don't feel so bad about it today, just last night I was thinking to much, so it kept me awake."

"If it helps you any, know that I am praying for the two of you."

"That does help a great deal. I am thankful that God is going to use us to help others out, although I am not quite sure yet how he will do that."

April came walking down stairs. She smiled at her mom and dad.

"Good morning sweet heart." Her father said.

"Morning daddy, mama making you something to eat before you leave for work?"

"Yep, would you like to eat with me."

"Mama makes me pancakes, but I can have a piece of bacon with you."

"Okay, sit right next to your ole dad, and have a piece."

"April did you happen to notice if Jimmy is up yet?"

"I heard something when I walked by his room."

"Okay good. I hope he's up and getting dressed. I need to take him over to Rose's house before we go to the studio."

"Daddy, mama said that you're not coming with us today."

"Nope honey I'm not. I think that you and your mom are a lot better at this then I am. You and she did most of the talking last week, and you both know a great deal more about this sort of thing that I do."

"Will you watch us today?"

"Yes, honey I will. I don't know if you remember what my office looks like."

"Yes, I do remember it."

"Good, I have my tv in there, and I and the guys will be watching you and your mom today." He put his arm around her. "You know April, I am so very happy that you are here with us today. I just want you to know that I am very proud of you honey."

She looked at her dad and gave a slight grin. "Why are you proud of me." She didn't feel that someone should be proud of her, there were times that she struggled feeling unclean because others have touched her, even if it was against her will.

"Oh honey, you love others so much that you're willing to relive this terrible thing that has happened to you, just so you can help others. Not everyone would be willing to do that."

It made her happy to know that her father was proud of her.

"I love you daddy, you're not one of the bad guys, you're a good guy. Just like the black man that took me to the police station was."

"Thank you honey, I am not a bad guy, I hate what they do."

18

On the drive to the studio, Karen thought it would be a good time to talk with April. "Honey, you know when you told me yesterday that you wanted to tell the people watching us about the little boys that were raped."

"Yes mama."

"I'm not to sure if they will allow you to talk about their butts bleeding on tv."

"Why not mama, that's what happened.

"Well, when we go on television there are certain things that need to be said differently."

"Okay, mama will you tell me how to say it?"

"Let me think about it for a minute."

"Okay mama." She waited until her mother would let her know.

"I think if you feel strongly about telling them about the boys being raped. Maybe you should just say that they forced you to watch little boys being raped, without saying you seen them bleeding."

"Okay mama, but don't you think that I should talk about that?"

Karen thought for a minute, then she realized yes people need to be aware of that happening to the little boys that are sold into sex slavery. "Yes, honey I do think that people should be made aware of it."

They drove to the studio, all the while Karen prayed within her self about what she should say during her time talking. "Are you nervous about today honey?"

"No, I'm not mama?"

"That's good, I think today will be good for us. We must try and answer everyone that calls in their questions."

After arriving at the studio, Karen told April that she wanted them to say a quick prayer first before going inside. "Dear Lord, you know that we are here to help others see the light. I ask for wisdom in the words that are spoken by us. Help people receive healing and help today, amen."

"Amen." April spoke.

They got out of the car and walked up to the door where they were greeted by Mr. Chambers. "Hello, it is very nice to have you come and join me once again for my show. I think today is going to be a very good day, I'm sure that after all the people called in after the last show, we will have several callers calling in today to ask questions."

"That's great." Spoke Karen giving him a nice smile.

"Let's step on in and take our seats. Does anyone need to use the restroom first."

"No," neither of them needed too.

"Okay then let's take our seats, and I'm going to have the microphone hooked up on you. Last time you were here, we receive feedback on many that watched us."

"That's what my husband told me. That's great, we feel this sort of things needs the light shed on it. We need more help getting the children freed from these evil places."

"I completely agree, that is why I have invited you again, I just know that there is more that needs to be said."

They took their seats where they were asked to sit. A woman came up to them and placed a microphone on their shirt. "All set." She spoke.

"Okay are you ready, we will start in a moment."

"Yep, we are ready." Karen looked at April sitting straight up with a half-smile on her face. She looked to be a little nervous, although she said that she was not.

"We are here once again with the Davis family today. They were on here last Tuesday with us. We will be discussing the topic of Sex trafficking in with the children. My name is Jack Chambers, and this here is April and her mother Karen Davis." The camera was all on Karen and April.

"Last week we talked about how April had been kidnapped and sold into child sex slavery for a little over two years. She had just recently been returned back to her home over the last few months. I'd like April to speak with you all about what it was like for her when she was away from home. We are taking in callers to ask questions, but I will remind you, to be respectful." He told April to start talking.

"When I was not at home with my family, and men were raping me all day long most days, I used to dream about the day I would see my family again."

"Can you tell me, if any of the men that would rape you, came back a second time?"

Karen hated that he asked her that question, she was unsure what difference it meant if it was the same or different ones.

"Yes, many of the same ones came back."

"When they came back, what was it like for you to see the same ones?"

"I hated them, some would tell me that they will come back and then take me home to my mom and dad, but they only lied. They hurt me the same way as they did before."

"Was there a time that you never thought that you would be returning home?"

"Yes, a lot of times."

"Can you share with us, some of those times?"

"One time when Tina came in my room after I was crying because one of the guys that came in my room hurt me really bad. She told me that Kevin said that if I didn't stop fighting the men, that I would have to go hungry and never see my family again."

"We have a caller right now, go ahead caller, you have a question?"

It was a man's voice, it sounded very rough. "I'd like to ask April if at any time that when the men raped her, if she ever got used to it?"

Jack shallowed deep, looking at April. "April, I think what the caller means, was there a time that it stopped hurting you so much?" he did not like that caller's questions.

"It didn't hurt me like it did the first few times, but the pain was always there. They were evil men that did that to me and many others."

"I remind the callers to keep the questions repectful. "Karen was there ever a time that you never thought that you were going to see April again?" Jack asked.

"I think that there was a time I thought that could be the case. I tried to not think about that ever being the possibility, but as time went on, and I hadn't heard anything about her whereabouts, I began to wonder if I might never see her again."

More calls came in and the both of them gave the best answers that they could. Some of them were ones that they never cared for. There were questions that should have not have been asked. Like one of the callers had the nerve to ask April if she ever liked any of the men that came to her. Jack quickly rose to the occasion and told the caller that he needed to be ashamed of himself asking a little child, if she enjoyed being raped. He hung the call up on the caller, it literally made him upset to hear a grown man ask a question like that.

"I had to make a decision after our last caller that was so inappropriately had asked a child a question that was not necessary. Because of that caller, we will not be taking any more calls."

"Thank you." Karen spoke.

"Can I answer that man's question?" April spoke, which shocked her mom and Mr. Chambers.

Jack looked at Karen, he didn't know if he should allow April to answer it.

"Are you sure honey?" Karen asked her daughter.

"Yes, I'm sure mama."

"Okay, go ahead April, speak what's on your mind."

"I know that I am only nine years old, and when I was seven years old men started to rape me every day fifty-sixty times a day. Now I don't know anyone that would ask a man to do that to them let a lone a small child, that only knew that they should be at home with there family. I was a happy child when I was at home with my little brother and my mom and dad. My whole life was turned up-side down. I hated those men for what they did to me and raping the little boys and girls there every day. Some of the children died, and I wanted to die many times, like when they would bring two guys in my room at once to rape me. And I've learned a lot since all of that happened to me, and one thing I have learned is to get to know when a man is like those that raped me. And that man that asked me that horrible question, sounds like he would be one that enjoyed raping little children."

Karen and Jack never seen that coming, they were both stunned by her answer to the man.

"I want to say this to that man, shame on you and what you do. You are not a good person to ever ask a child that's been raped for two years if she enjoyed it." Karen spoke.

"Thank you, for that incredible answer. April, you amaze me, you have been through hell on earth and yet you sit here so grown up beyond years. I know that it did not come easy for you to get there. But through it all, you have found the need to help others, and also to expose those that are like that too. Thank you, for coming on my show, so young that you are, but yet so much more grown up then some of the callers that have called in."

On the drive home, Karen didn't really know what to say to April about that man that called in and asked her a terrible unappropriated question. She waited to hear April talk to her.

"Mama."

"Yes honey."

"Are you mad at me?"

"No honey, why would you ask me that?"

"Because you are quiet."

"Oh honey, there are just times that people remain quiet and feel no need to talk."

"Okay, can I talk then?"

Karen chuckled; she was always being surprised by some of the things that her daughter would say. "Yes, honey you can talk all you want too."

"I think that man that called, is like Kevin. He was not a good man mama."

Karen listened to her daughter express her feelings, she wondered if there was a way, she could tell that just by hearing the man talk and ask her that question. "Do you really believe so?"

"Yes, mama I do."

"What makes you so sure about it honey?"

"Because when some of the men that came in my room, they would ask me the same thing."

Karen felt like something just punched her in her gut. She wanted to cry at that time, but she knew that she needed to be strong for April. "Oh, honey those men that asked you that were sick in the head. They are gross and I'm glad they are in prison now."

"Mama, they aren't in prison."

Karen looked at April. "What are you saying honey, remember when we went to court, they all got many years in prison."

"Mama, they were the ones that got money to see me, they beat me up to make me do what they wanted. But mama, all the other men are still out there, to rape other children. They were not in court. Maybe just a few of them, but most they were not."

Karen couldn't believe how she never thought about that, her mind was so much on putting Kevin and his men away, those that worked for him, that she never thought about all the men that paid money to rape her daughter and the other children. How could she had not thought about that, of course there are so many of them, how would she ever be able to find out who they were so they too could go to prison for rape. "That's true honey, there are so many of them, I wouldn't even know where to begin to find all of them." The thoughts of all the men that took part in raping her daughter were still out there to rape other children. What could she possibly do to catch these evil men, that got their thrills on preying on the young and innocent children. She knew that something must happen in the whole world to stop this sex trafficking of the children.

Later when Micah came home, April and Jimmy were outside playing in the back yard. Micah could see that Karen looked very disappointed. "What's wrong honey, you don't seem to be very happy. Tell me was it the man that called the studio and said that crazy remark to April?"

"That man was just wicked to ask a little girl that has been traumatized something like that. Making rape of a small child into a fantasy. No, that's not it, I already got past that."

"Okay, then what is it."

"It's something that I am very angry with myself. April said something to me on our way home, that I just can't believe I never even really paid attention too."

"Honey please will you tell me what you are talking about, stop beating around the bush. Now come on honey."

"April and I were talking when she mentioned to me that the man that called in was like Kevin."

"I heard her say that he was like the men that had her."

"What you didn't hear is her tell me that the men that did this to her are still out raping other children."

"Why would she say that?"

"Because it is true, Kevin and his men may be in prison, but what about all the other men that came there and paid big money to rape our daughter, where are they at? I will tell you where they are at, they are still out there to rape other children that have not been rescued. They are running free to lure other children into a sex rings."

Micah could understand why his wife was so upset. "I know that honey, and I hate it too, but we can only take down the big ring of them that hold the children against their will. It's the cries of the unknown that hurts me so much. There are so many places out there that are holding hundreds of children to be sold for sex. If we could bring down those places, then we will start putting an end to the men going to pay money for them. Remember when the Sargant told us that his men where still at Kevin's arresting the men that were coming there to rape the children, that day they picked up April."

"I remember, but you know that only lasted that day. Where does one even start, there are so many places and they are all over the place. At least when Trump was in office, he was bringing a lot of those places down. I remember watching several places that people were selling children for sex being caught. Even today I was reading when I was at work, that a man and women were caught into sex trafficking, and now there are going away for a long time."

"I wish I could do more to get them caught, I hate the evil of man's heart. I just don't understand that some of these perverts are fathers to little boys and girls, some are grandpas, uncles. How they can even live with themselves to do such evil to little children in beyond me."

"They are very evil to commit such things like that on little children. It's like they have no conscience on what they are doing."

"I don't think that they have, just like the pastor was saying on Sunday, man has become evil minded. They run to and fro, like the devil seeking who they can bring harm too."

"That's true, we just don't know who we can trust anymore. I was reading where a pastor was also raping a little girl that went to his church. It went on for years and the little girl's parents was still going to the church and they didn't even know about it."

"Oh my gosh, so how did anyone find out about him and what he was doing?"

"The girl that he had been raping since she was ten years old, is now sixteen years old and she finally came out with the truth and told her family what's been going on."

"Oh, dear Lord, when the pastors are raping the children, we know that we can't trust others. They went to his church for all of those years and they never knew it right under their nose."

"Just terrible this kind of thing can happen within the church. God help us to know who are the people that are hurting our children."

19

Days had gone by since Karen and April had last gone to the studio. Mr. Chambers has called to let them know that they were sorry about having the lines open to receive calls from others.

Micah had let him know that his wife was not interested in coming back if they were going to have the lines open for callers to speak rude to their daughter.

"Mr. Davis, I am truly sorry for that, and I'd love to have them come back on again. I had already taken the liberty of speaking with my producer about the phone calls. Now he has asked me to call you up and let you know that nothing like that will ever happen again. I think he thought that after what your daughter had went through, that people would be more mindful of the trauma she had."

"I will speak with my wife, and see how she feels about coming on your show again, and I will let you know."

"I will be having a show tomorrow about a father that is divorced and his x-wife is having their son go through transitioning against his will and the sons will that is only a seven-year-old little boy. He has told his father that he doesn't want to be a little girl, but the court went with what the mother wanted for him, they didn't care less about what the child wants or the father."

"What in the world is it coming to that a judge would side with the parent that wants this kind of evil to happen to her child?"

"Yes, I know, that is why I am having these kinds of talk shows, I want the truth of the corruption to come out, and hopefully put an end to this madness. Will you talk with your wife and ask her to give us another chance. If she is willing, we would like her on next Tuesdays again. And please let her know to watch tomorrows show."

"I will let her know and I will get back with you."

Micah called up his wife, he didn't think that she wanted to go back and do another episode, but he did tell Mr. Chambers that he would ask her. "Guess what honey."

"What?"

"Mr. Chambers just called."

"I don't think so honey, what them callers did was not right, and I don't ever want to put April through that again."

"That's just what I told him, but he had said they will not have any callers. Oh yeah, he also told me that he would like you to make sure that you watch his show tomorrow."

"Why?"

"After what he told me I think you should watch it too honey. There is an evil what is happening to the children. Right now, he will be having a father of a little seven-year-old boy on there."

"What about the father of the boy?"

"His x wife is having the little boy changed into a girl."

"Oh, dear Lord, such evil of a mother to do that to her own little boy."

"Yeah, it sure is, and the father took her to court I guess but the judge told him he will allow the x wife to do what she plans for the boy."

"We are living with very wicked people in this world. It's just terrible a judge that is supposed to protect us is allowing a child to have a sex change."

"You can let Mr. Chamber know, that as long as there will be no phone callers allowed on the show, April and I will come in. And also tell him that I will be watching his show tomorrow."

"Okay if you are really sure."

"Yes, honey, I am sure. If his show is getting that much exposer, then it must be making some kind of head waves."

"Okay I will call him up, I'll see you tonight."

"See you tonight."

Karen thought about what her husband told her about the father of the boy. Her heart ached for him, knowing what it must be like, knowing that your child was about to not remain a son anymore, all because two evil people made a choice for him. Such wicked hearted people that will have a little child change from who God created them to be. *"God help that father, help the little boy not to have that done to him."* She cried out to God.

The next day Karen made sure to watch Jack Chambers tv show. She wanted to see the father who was fighting the court for his son not to be changed from a boy to a girl.

As she sat down watching the show, she listened to the father's horror story about what a wicked woman his x wife was. She didn't care less that her son didn't want to be a girl, he said that he wanted to be a boy and play baseball, but she never cared and the judge never cared.

She moved away without the father's permission, to have their son changed into a little girl. He cried while talking to Jack on the show. She could tell that he had a real fathers love for his son, she was unsure what was going on in the boy's mothers head. One thing she was sure of, is that the mother did not understand what real love even was.

Karen and April did another tv show, she was able to speak more about the trauma that her daughter had gone through. April spoke more about the abuse of the men that raped her, and what kind of men they were. She exposed the truth that some of the men, were doctors, lawyers, judges. She let people know that it doesn't matter what they did for a living, what matter was what their heart was like.

She told of how many of the men, forced her into having oral sex with them. How they stole her innocence and all the other children that were there.

Over the course of a few months, April and Karen were invited to speak in schools and in churches. April was no longer going to see Ellie; her mind was all about helping other as much as she could. There were still some moments where she would sit in silence and stay to herself, but those times were short lived. The more she opened up about what she had gone through was all the more she herself was being healed from the hurt and pain. She slowly began to forgive the men that had raped her and abused her badly. She talked about it to many young girls and their parents. As she did, she seen some of them learn to come out of the shell they were put into where now they could sit and talk to their family members about the ordeal they had gone through at the hands of evil men and women. April had a book written about her life; it was called "Cries of the Unknown." People were buying that book all over.

Karen's deepest thoughts and wishes is that everyone will be made more aware of the evil that awaits to prey upon the innocence of the children. She said pray each day, and ask God to cover your children with the blood of Jesus. Watch your children closer than you had before, look for the signs that someone may have abused them. She ends with a prayer for everyone.

"Dear Lord, we humbly ask that you will wrap your arms around each child. That you will cover them with the blood of Jesus. That nothing will harm them and we will be made more aware of the danger that lurks out there to harm our children. That wisdom will live and dwell inside of us, and most of all that we will surrender our whole lives over to you, Amen."

Printed by Libri Plureos GmbH in Hamburg, Germany